They Die Strangers

Modern Middle East
Literatures in Translation
Series

They Die Strangers

Mohammad Abdul-Wali

Translated by
Abubaker Bagader and Deborah Akers

Introduction by
Shelagh Weir

Center for Middle Eastern Studies
The University of Texas at Austin

Library of Congress Control Number: 20010966341
ISBN: 0-292-70508-5

Printed in the United States of America
Cover photograph by Carel Bertram
Cover design: Diane Watts
Series editor: Annes McCann-Baker

The Center gratefully acknowledges financial support for the publication
of *They Die Strangers* from the National Endowment for the Arts in
Washington, D.C.

CONTENTS

Introduction   *page 1*

❧ Novella ❧

They Die Strangers   *page 17*

❧ Stories ❧

The Ghoul   *page 69*

Brother, Are You Going To Fight Them All   *page 75*

Ya Khabiir   *page 79*

The Chinese Road   *page 83*

Nothing New   *page 89*

The Land, Salma   *page 95*

The Color of Rain   *page 101*

Saturday Market   *page 109*

Abu Rupee   *page 113*

The Slap   *page 119*

The Last Class   *page 123*

A Woman   *page 127*

On the Road to Asmara   *page 131*

Translators' Dedication

This book is dedicated to Raad Shubaily, Deborah's son; and to Ahmad Bagader, Abubaker's son. Their bonds with both the east and the west truly embody the spirit of our work.

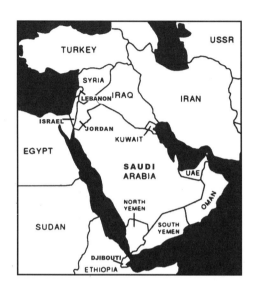

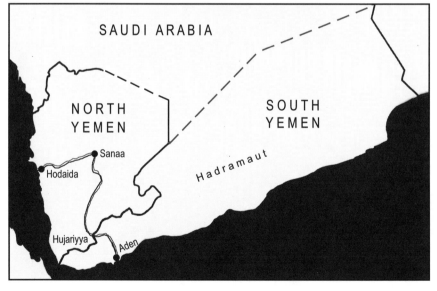

Yemen during the period of
Abdul-Wali's stories (1950s – 1960s)

Introduction

Mohammad Abdul-Wali is admired in his paternal homeland of North Yemen[1] as a pioneer of fiction writing. Prior to the 1960s, when his stories were first published, the literature of North Yemen mainly consisted of works of religious scholarship, histories, geographies, and biographies that looked to the past and idealized the achievements of the political and religious elite. Abdul-Wali's work marked a radical break from these traditional genres by focussing on contemporary themes, and by describing with vivid and compassionate realism the lives of ordinary people, especially the oppressed and socially marginal. This focus must first be understood in relationship to Abdul-Wali's own social background and tragically brief life.

Mohammad Ahmad Abdul-Wali[2] was born in Ethiopia in 1940, and spent his childhood there. His mother was Ethiopian, and his father, Ahmad, was an émigré from North Yemen. His background made the author a *muwallad*, or "person of mixed blood." This birth status undoubtedly sensitized Abdul-Wali to the race issue, which is a subtext in several stories where skin color is mentioned, and is a major theme in the two stories in which muwallads prominently figure ("On the Road to Asmara," and "They Die Strangers").

Ahmad Abdul-Wali, who was probably a shopkeeper, endeavored to maintain his son's Muslim and Yemeni identity in the Christian-African environment of Ethiopia. He sent him to the Yemeni Community School in Addis Ababa, where two of the stories here appear to be set. Then in 1954, when his son was about fourteen, he sent him to an institute for Islamic studies in Aden in South Yemen,[3] and married him to his cousin. (Cousin marriage is common in Yemen, as is marriage near puberty.) This was Abdul-Wali's first encounter with Yemen and its conditions. It was at around this time, in his middle teens, that he claims to have begun writing.

In 1955, Abdul-Wali went to Cairo, where he attended colleges (one a school of Al-Azhar University) and developed Marxist sympathies. The latter is consistent with the passionate and idealistic preoccupation with social and political injustice in his writings, and helps us understand his subsequent turbulent career. He was expelled from Egypt for political reasons, visited Yemen again, then went to Moscow where he learned Russian and attended a literature course at the Gorki Institute. When the republican revolution took place in Yemen in late 1962, he returned to his country and joined the diplomatic service of the newly created Yemen Arab Republic, serving as Chargé d'Affaires in Moscow, then in East Berlin until he was expelled for allegedly spying in 1967. Back in Yemen, which was still in a state of civil war, he was briefly Director General of Aviation. Thereafter, he fell out with his government politically and spent two long stints in prison. After his second incarceration he fled to Aden, which was by then under a Marxist regime.[4]

In 1973, Abdul-Wali was killed in a plane crash while flying from Aden to Hadramaut in South Yemen with a group of Yemeni intellectuals and politicians. He left a Swedish wife, whom he had married after the death of his Yemeni wife, and several children.

The stories collected in this volume are all set either in Ethiopia or in North Yemen, specifically in or near the Hujariyyah in the south where his father originated. Their principal themes are the difficult political conditions in Yemen in the 1950s and 1960s, and the problems of long-term emigration. To appreciate the stories fully, it is therefore also necessary to understand something of this background.

The Hujariyyah is a mountainous region of farmers and traders in the far south of North Yemen. From the late nineteenth century, the Hujariyyah was the main area of emigration from North Yemen—mainly because of local poverty and the proximity of the port of Aden, only one long day's walk away. Most men left to seek work, and some to escape political oppression. The majority of migrants were uneducated, took unskilled jobs in Aden itself, and returned home regularly for Muslim festivals and other important events. Others took menial jobs on ships and were often at sea for years. And some, mainly single, men settled permanently abroad—in ports where their ships had docked or in cities where they could work in industry or trade. Men lived frugally abroad, and most remitted as much as they could to support the families they had left behind and to finance capital projects such as house-building or setting-up shops back in their villages. The whole point of enduring the usually gruelling work and long separations was to help those left behind. As a result of generations of emigration, there are communities of expatriate North Yemenis throughout the Middle East and in France, England, Wales, the USA, and Ethiopia.[5]

In the 1930s, when Abdul-Wali's father Ahmad presumably emigrated to Ethiopia. The ruler of North Yemen, the Zaydi imam[6] Yahya Hamiid al-Diin, was ruthlessly consolidating his state in the aftermath of the Ottoman occupation (which ended in 1918). The imam employed especially harsh taxation and policing methods in the southern, Shaafi`ii (Sunni) part of his domain, including the Hujariyyah. The inhabitants of the Hujariyyah lacked the strong tribal organization of the north or powerful leaders, and could not resist the brutalities of Zaydi rule. But resentment grew, and in the late 1930s, leading Hujariyyans helped found The Free Yemeni Movement (FYM), referred to in the stories as The Liberals Party.[7] This loose association opposed Imam Yahya's isolationist policies, and pressed for political reform and economic change in North Yemen, which was then almost totally undeveloped. Most of the population lived in squalid conditions in small, scattered villages without running water, electricity, or modern educational and health facilities, and all travel was on foot or by animal. The FYM's mainly intellectual activities were partly financed by contributions from expatriate Yemenis, including those across the Red Sea in Ethiopia as mentioned in *They Die Strangers.*, and Abdul-Wali's father was a supporter.

Imam Yahya was assassinated in 1948,[8] but the situation in Yemen improved little under the rule (1948-62) of his son and successor, Imam Ahmad, who perpetuated his father's strict policies. He did, however, agree to a few development projects being effected with foreign aid. The most spectacular of these was the construction of the first surfaced road in Yemen, which was built by the Chinese and climbed from the port of Hodeidah on the Red Sea coast (Tihamah) through steep, rugged mountains to the capital, Sanaa, on the high plateau. This extraordinary engineering feat, which Abdul-Wali perhaps saw during his first visit to Yemen in the 1950s, figures in "The Chinese Road."

In 1962, the thousand-year-old Zaydi imamate was finally overthrown in a military coup, and the Yemen Arab Republic was established. There followed eight years of civil war between republicans and royalists in which the republicans were victorious. Revolution also took place in South Yemen. The British left in 1967 and were replaced by the Marxist People's Democratic Republic of Yemen. In 1990, North and South Yemen unified to create the present Republic of Yemen.

The stories translated in this volume have a strong autobiographical feel. Most are written in the first person by a male narrator, and all describe situations which Abdul-Wali probably personally experienced, observed, or heard about firsthand.

These are intimate tales. Most focus on one main character or two usually contrasting characters, and describe a single main event or encounter. Much use is made of dialogue to expose ideas and feelings, and of weather to create mood and reflect emotions. And the stories are set in vividly drawn landscapes and places. All this gives them a powerful sense of immediacy and authenticity. The reader should bear in mind, however, that Abdul-Wali mainly wanted to spotlight people in forlorn or stressful circumstances, and he does so extremely movingly, but he thereby leaves much in the dark. He ignores the variegated nature of Yemeni and Ethiopian society. He also focuses on individuals to the exclusion of their social nexus, leading to a distorted depiction of their situations. It is striking, for example, that the stories set in Addis Ababa give scarcely a glimpse of its cosmopolitan life, and that most of the Ethiopian characters in the stories are prostitutes. It could be argued that it was Yemenis not Africans he chiefly wanted to depict, but here too he bends reality to his purpose. In "Nothing New" and "The Land, Salma," for example, he portrays village

4

women as lonely and socially isolated because their husbands are away. This ignores the fact that Yemeni village women are supported by dense networks of relatives and neighbors, and lead intense social lives among themselves, regardless of the presence or absence of their husbands. Yemeni men abroad and at home are also part of active communities, and spend much time in social gatherings, often chewing *qat*.[9] Also conspicuous by their absence are joyful or family events, or the exuberance and sense of humor that are such dominant features of Yemeni culture. The melancholy, brooding loners who people these stories should not, therefore, be taken in any sense as "typical" Yemenis.

Abdul-Wali was primarily writing for fellow Yemenis, who would have implicitly understood his often subtle cultural and political references and the contexts of his stories. However, they require some explanation for western readers unfamiliar with Yemen.

The first eight of the stories collected in this volume are set in Yemen. The first story, "The Ghoul," relates a fable that invites an obvious political interpretation and sets the scene for the others. The ghoul, or evil spirit, who lives in the mountain cave and terrorizes the village surely symbolizes the imam of North Yemen and the despotic imamate (especially since the last imam, al-Badr, was sheltered in caves during the civil war). If so, then the ghoul's destruction at the hands of the poor, brave mariner's widow represents the demolition of the imamate in the republican revolution of 1962. And the revival of her sick son—"the man of tomorrow"—by the ghoul's gory death, must symbolize Yemen's renaissance as a republic.

The arrogant policeman in "Brother, Are You Going to Fight Them All?", with his gun slung over his shoulder, traditional clothing, and bare feet, represents one of the northern tribesmen whom the Hamiid al-Diin imams employed as mercenaries to enforce their rule in southern Shaafi'ii areas such as the Hujariyyah. Southerners feared and detested these men, whose religious and social loyalties lay elsewhere, and who were sometimes brutal. But their harsh methods ultimately derived from the government. One of the most deeply resented was the obligation to extract their daily wages from the people they were sent to deal with, regardless of the latter's guilt or innocence.[10] These are the "dues" demanded in the story.

In "Ya Khabiir," we meet a similarly attired, barefoot soldier chewing qat. He is identified as being from the tribal region of Hashid, but this story undermines and softens the southern stereotype of the fierce northern tribesman. Where the other is portrayed as an anonymous executor of the arbitrary cruelty of government power, this one is humanized and made a mouthpiece for discontent with the imamate. The soldier chases after a lawyer walking home through the mountains. The lawyer fears the worst because of the brutality his village has experienced from his kind, but the soldier just wants a companion. He guides the lawyer along the path, and on the way helps him understand that he is a victim as well as an instrument of the system. He explains that he was forced into this work because *shaykhs* (tribal leaders) took his land, and complains that he has not seen his family for years. He also denies that all soldiers loot and steal, and points out that the Governor takes more than they (meaning in taxes). By dusk the men are friends and pray together, and the soldier cracks a self-deprecating joke, forbidding the lawyer to tell anyone that a soldier forced him to pray at gunpoint.

"The Color of Rain" takes place in the mountains of southern Yemen during the 1962–70 civil war. Two contrasting Yemeni characters sit admiring the moonlit scenery. One, the narrator, is a young man from Aden, who shivers in the unaccustomed cold, and thinks longingly of the bride he has left in the care of his family. He is a novice fighter, and scared. His companion is a lonely old salt, toughened by twenty years of laboring on ships and in mines and fighting for the Italians and British (in the Second World War). During the story, a brief, shockingly violent incident occurs which scarcely interrupts the men's musings or the reader's reading. We are thus made complicit in the casual, anonymous cruelty of war.

"The Saturday Market" is set before the departure of the British from South Yemen. A young man is journeying from Aden to the Hujariyyah to celebrate a Muslim festival (*eid*) with his wife and new baby, born while he was abroad. His car has broken down, so he is travelling on foot (like generations of migrant workers returning home, though this is not said). The landscape is beautiful and the mountains of the Hujariyyah beckon. He arrives at a busy market on the border between South and North Yemen, and surveys the hills of the Subayhi "tribesmen." A British flag flies from a nearby guard-post, and he remembers the Subayhis they have shot, and how revenge shootings continue still.[11] His reverie ends, and he is overwhelmed by the sights, sounds, and smells of the market, which stoke his anxiety to get home. "Black" faces are mentioned, who are peddlers of African ancestry. Rutting male donkeys are untied and allowed to get at their mates. Their female keeper glances at him suggestively, then leaves. A dancer from Tihamah arouses his lust and self-disgust. The sun beats mercilessly down. It all becomes too much. When the market ends at midday, people leave with their bundles. But he remains, still wondering how to get home. The evocation of volatile emotions and desperate, impotent entrapment suggests that this tale might be an allegory of prison life.

In "The Chinese Road," Abdul-Wali views this momentous engineering project through the incredulous eyes of a naive laborer in Tihamah. He watches the Chinese affectionately, marvelling as they nimbly scale the heights and explode mountains to drive the road through to Sanaa. And he compares them favorably to the other foreigners he has worked for— the red-faced people (i.e. Western development experts) who slept in tents, drank a lot and "took notes," but achieved nothing. He has never been to Sanaa, but we know he soon will. The first roads changed more than the revolution.

The last two stories based in Yemen return to the theme of long-term emigration, and take a female perspective on the plight of wives left behind in their villages while their men work abroad. Layla's husband, in "Nothing New," has been away a year working in American coal mines. She longs for his return, but fears his ship has sunk in the war (presumably the Second World War), or that he has found another wife. His remittances have dried up, taxes and poor harvests have impoverished her, and she is exhausted from caring for the fields and animals and their baby son. Her cousin is better off because her husband is only in Aden. Then the camel caravan arrives from Aden (this is before roads), bearing letters, gifts, and money from her husband. But other waiting women get nothing, presaging the heart-rending ending.

In "The Land, Salma," Abdul-Wali uses a disembodied voice to interrogate the heroine and reveal her innermost feelings. Salma's husband has been overseas for five years, and has only returned once to impregnate her with a son he does not even know about. Salma worries, like Layla, that her husband might marry someone else and never return. Like many women in the Hujariyyah, she is doing traditionally "male" tasks on top of "female" household chores in the absence of her man, and is disappointed that her working life did not improve after she joined her husband's family at marriage. She also worries about ageing, and fantasizes about illicit love. But she finally finds comfort and salvation in her devotion to the land.

The rest of the stories are based in Ethiopia, and view long-term emigration from the émigré's perspective. Four are cameos of expatriate Yemeni children's lives in Addis Ababa. Both "Abu Rupee" and "The Slap" are narrated by an eleven-year-old boy called Sa'id who attends "the community school." "Abu Rupee" describes Sa'id's awakening by a misfit. The boy dreams of becoming a merchant and helping the poor. Then he befriends Abu Rupee, a wise fool who wanders the streets drawing caricatures on walls for a rupee. Abu Rupee scorns money and despises his fellow Yemenis who have abandoned their country and women to seek wealth. Merchants forget their youthful ideals, he says, and let their poor (like him) be derided by the foreigners they live among. Overcome by nostalgia, he draws the boy a picture of Yemen and extols its beauty and famous past, urging him to go there. The boy decides to become an artist, and Abu Rupee disappears. The story concludes with a poignant re-encounter in Aden, five years later.

In "Abu Rupee," Sa'id's father is in the background, doing the accounts; in "The Slap," he is cutting up cardboard to cover notebooks he sells. Sa'id infuriates him by giving an Ethiopian customer too much change. He angrily reminds his son how lucky he is to be supported and getting an education, when *he*, by contrast, had to support his parents and left his country to improve his son's prospects. Sa'id has obviously heard all this before. He is more worried about whether he can persuade his father to pay for a uniform he must wear at school for the anniversary of Emperor Haile Selassie's coronation.

"The Last Class," like "Abu Rupee," is about losing a treasured relationship and longing for the homeland. A class of boys in fifth grade are stunned at the imminent loss of a beloved Yemeni teacher who made them love and yearn for the country they have never seen. "A Woman" is about adolescent sexual desire. The fourteen-year-old narrator walks through a red-light district in Addis Ababa, and is inflamed by an Ethiopian prostitute who bestows on him a free kiss. Abdul-Wali uses African prostitutes in several stories to represent the moral danger, as he sees it, of expatriate life in Ethiopia, and portrays them as jolly, sassy, blatantly erotic women in charge of their lives, in contrast to Yemeni village women whom he depicts as sad, repressed, abandoned victims.

The remaining stories focus on experiences and encounters of different types of Yemeni men. "On the Road to Asmara" is about the difficulty of maintaining Yemeni identity in Africa. The narrator is a Yemeni muwallad stuck waiting for transport in a flyblown Ethiopian settlement of shacks and bars that grew up to service the Italians and is now in decline. He fends off prostitutes and falls into conversation with a Yemeni shopkeeper chewing qat like himself. Each evaluates the other's situation. The shopkeeper guesses the narrator is a muwallad, and envies him belonging to Africa by birth. The narrator, for his part, is appalled at the way the shopkeeper's Yemeni identity is fading away. The latter admits that, after thirty years in Ethiopia, he is probably forgotten back in Yemen. He is also letting his muwallad children lose their Muslim religion. He has sent them to a Christian school, and they can only speak Amharic, the main language in Ethiopia. And he is even starting to forget his Arabic.

The Yemeni shopkeeper, Abdou Sa'id, who is the central character of the novella *They Die Strangers*, provides a striking contrast to the shopkeeper stranded on the road to Asmara. Where the latter has lost his connections with Yemen and assimilated, Abdou Sa'id has struggled to maintain his links with Yemen, where he left a wife (whose face he cannot remember) and child, and devotes his life to the dream of returning in triumph as a wealthy man. He works nonstop, and lives in squalor in the back of his shop in Addis Ababa so he can send all his profits home. By the time we first meet him, over ten years into his sojourn, his remittances have paid for a magnificent house to be built back in his village. His obsession with his goal makes him shun any relationships that might enmesh him in the local community, including those with Yemenis; he does not even contribute, like others, to The Free Yemeni Movement (the Liberals Party). His only human contacts are over the counter with customers, and with dispensable sexual partners. Unlike the Yemenis in the other stories, who resist the allure of African women and hate themselves for being tempted, he is an uninhibited, guilt-free satyr, notorious for sleeping with local prostitutes and fathering children he never acknowledges. Even his one regular relationship, with the rich wife of an important official, is self-ish—for the tax-man is after him and she might get her husband to intercede.

One day an event occurs that threatens all his plans. The Muslim mother of one of his bastards dies, and her Christian friend, also a prostitute as the mother had been, begs Abdou Sa'id to accept responsibility for his destitute son. Despite the fact that she once gave him her virginity, and that as a Muslim he has a duty to prevent his son being raised by Christians and among prostitutes, he refuses her blandishments. In desperation, she asks a Yemeni *sayyid* (descendant of the Prophet Muhammad) to intercede. Abdou Sa'id now takes some sideswipes at the pretensions and self-interested manipulations of the religious elite. The sayyid seizes the chance to enhance his own reputation for piety and closeness to God, while delegating the actual hard work of dealing with the problem to a *hajji* (one who has visited Mecca). He thus preserves his own superior detachment from the world, and continues to sit in self-imposed confinement, receiving the gifts people lavish on him in gratitude for his religious services. He tells the hajji, a pillar of the local Yemeni community, that he has learned about this problem directly from God, and that He wants the hajji to be His instrument in persuading Abdou Sa'id to do his religious duty. The self-important hajji is ecstatic to receive this honor, and bustles about in search of the culprit. One of the rare comic moments in the book is when he bursts in on an acquaintance of Abdou Sa'id, who assumes the hajji is hunting for subscriptions to the Liberal Party again. When he eventually tracks him down, he also fails to move the flinty Abdou Sa'id, who decides to bring forward his long-cherished plan and escape immediately to Yemen. But (divine?) punishment foils him, and the boy is saved (and Abdou Sa'id's sins are redeemed) by the hajji's saintly assistant.

They Die Strangers is Abdul-Wali's most cautionary and didactic tale. Like many of the stories in this collection, it dwells on the negative aspects of long-term emigration: the anguish of long separations from families and homeland, the loneliness and moral hazards of living in an alien culture, and the tension between the emigrant's desire to assimilate in the host country and his yearning to return. But, where other characters strive to preserve their Yemeni identity and Muslim values in the context of an African and Christian environment, and regret their lapses and compromises, Abdou Sa'id emphatically does neither. He is an extreme example of a "fallen" émigré who ruthlessly betrays the ideals of his native culture and religion without remorse, fatally corrupted by his selfish, materialistic goal. By inflicting on him such a tragic end and denying him absolution, Abdul-Wali delivers an uncompromising verdict on the dangers and delusions, as he saw them, of Yemeni men living abroad alone.

Shelagh Weir

---

[1] By North Yemen I refer to the region which was the Mutawakkilite Kingdom of Yemen until the overthrow of its theocratic rulers, the Hamiid al-Diin imams, in the republican coup of 1962, when it became The Yemen Arab Republic.

[2] I have derived most of the following biographical information about Abdul-Wali from Günther Orth's well-researched introduction to his book on the modern Yemeni short story: *"Di Farbe des Regens": Entstehung und Entwicklung der modernen jemenitischen Kurzgeschichte*, Berlin: Klaus Schwarz Verlag, 1997, 80-83. I am grateful to Iris Glosemeyer for alerting me to the existence of this book, and for kindly sending me photocopies of

the latter pages. In the rest of his book, which I have been unable to see, Orth discusses nine of Abdul-Wali's short stories, including four that are included in this volume ("Abu Rupee," "The Land, Salma," "The Color of Rain," and "On the Road to Asmara"). I also obtained biographical information from the translators of this volume, and from Salma Jayyusi's *The Literature of Modern Arabia,* Austin: University of Texas Press, 1988.

[3] By South Yemen I mean what was at that time the British-controlled Aden Protectorates, and later became the People's Democratic Republic of Yemen. The institute was founded by Muhammad Salim al-Bayhani, a graduate of al-Azhar University in Cairo and a leading religious scholar in Aden in the 1950s. The institute closed in 1967 (See Abdullah Ahmed Muheirez, "Cultural Development in the People's Democratic Republic of Yemen," in B. R. Pridham (ed), *Economy, Society and Culture in Contemporary Yemen,* London: Croom Helm, 1985, 209).

[4] The People's Democratic Republic of Yemen.

[5] For an account of Yemeni communities in Britain, see Fred Halliday, *Arabs in Exile: Yemeni Migrants in Urban Britain,* London: I.B.Taurus, 1992. For Yemenis in the USA, see Jonathan Friedlander (ed), *Sojourners and Settlers: the Yemeni Immigrant Experience,* Salt Lake City: University of Utah Press, 1988.

[6] Zaydism is a branch of Shi'ah Islam, and the religious and temporal rulers of the Zaydi state in Yemen were entitled *imam.*

[7] See J. Leigh Douglas, *The Free Yemeni Movement: 1935-1962,* Beirut: American University in Beirut, 1987.

[8] Members of the Free Yemeni Movement were involved in plotting Imam Yahya's assassination in 1948, and in the military coup of 1962.

[9] *Qat* is a mildly stimulant leaf chewed by most Yemenis in afternoon social gatherings, and by travellers and workers to increase their alertness

(see Shelagh Weir, *Qat in Yemen: Consumption and Social Change*, British Museum Press, 1985). Abdul-Wali uses qat to symbolize Yemeni identity in several stories.

[10] This notorious system of punitive policing and billeting was called *tanfidh*.

[11] The Subayhis live in the hills and coastal plain south of the old border between North and South Yemen, and their territory is traversed by trade routes between Aden and the Hujariyyah. The Subayhis looted caravans and traded in arms activities, which the British and their local allies tried to control or suppress by force of arms (see R. J. Gavin, *Aden Under British Rule: 1839-1967*, London: Hurst, 1975*)*.

Novella

They Die Strangers

The only thing people of Sodset Kilo and the Marqatah in Addis Ababa knew about Abdou Sa'id was that he had opened his little store there more than ten years earlier. He, on the other hand, knew everything about the people who lived in the quarter, especially in the area where the neighborhood streets were always muddy from the constant rain, where in the winter intoxicating music played all night long, and hundreds of laborers and unemployed men sat guzzling Taja, the local alcoholic drink, while ogling prostitutes who had spent at least forty years in the business. Saturday was a stage on which the same performance was held week after week, to the point that Abdou knew what would happen even before it took place.

As for the quarter's residents, they loved him, but why? They did not know themselves. Perhaps they loved him because he was kinder than the other shopkeepers. Or perhaps it was his smile, the way it remained permanently fixed on his face, even when he seemed sad. He had lived there for ten years and still looked young, his expression was a constant mask of affability. How old was he? No one asked him, and even if they had, they would have found that he himself didn't know.

Sodset Kilo was the quarter of both rich men and slaves. It was the quarter of small, elegant villas with perpetually green gardens, the quarter of princely palaces, the quarter of the zoo, where one could hear the roar of lions competing with the shouts of drunkards. Sometimes it was a quiet quarter, like the gardens in the heart of the capital city. And sometimes it was as boisterous as wine gurgling out of barrels into stomachs that were never filled, no matter how much they drank.

Abdou cared nothing about all this. He lived among them but apart, like the distance between his dirty black clothes and his smiling white face. His shop was like a small room, ten meters long and three meters wide, but it was not just a shop; it was also where he lived. On the front shelves he had piled cheap goods right alongside expensive ones—rice, oil, honey, silk shirts, buttons, needles: everything the villa residents needed. Behind all these goods, tucked out of sight, was his bed. It was a strange kind of bed, consisting of some wooden boxes, a half-decayed mattress, and a blanket he had bought from the surplus left by the British army when they had tried to occupy Ethiopia. In one corner sat a stove, a large cooking pot, a teapot, and an old box. Inside the box was a suit he'd bought eight years earlier. He wore it on special holidays or whenever he went to Marqatah-Hamann to buy supplies for his shop.

In back of the shop was a small door, so low that Abdou Sa'id had to crouch down to about a half of his height to pass through it out into a small yard where he could relieve himself, and to a modest garden where he had planted tomatoes and green peppers. The yard was more organized and more beautiful than the area he called his room. A considerable amount of effort had gone into this yard and into the surrounding fence, which Abdou had built himself. He stayed home on Fridays, giving himself a couple of hours of leisure in which to work on his garden and to mend what the children from the quarter had ruined. Everyone called him "Camel Jockey," a term they used for all the Yemeni immigrants. This didn't disturb him as it did others. He responded to the slur with a friendly smile. Sometimes they called him "Saleh," though the name registered on his passport was "Abdou Sa'id." That didn't bother him either. Why should it? A name was a name, so long as they bought all they needed from his store. His tolerance attracted many customers . Maids from the villas refused to go to the Armenian shopkeeper's modern well-equipped store to buy what they needed, preferring instead to shop at Abdou's rat hole.

Each morning at six he finished his dawn prayers, put a pot of tea on his old kerosene stove, and opened his shop, reciting verses from the Quran and some prayers he had memorized as a child. He shooed away flies with an old feather fan, scattering dust, which shimmered in the first golden rays of the sun. If someone entered while he was eating a piece of bread or taking a sip of his morning tea, he dropped whatever he was doing in order to wait on the customer.

"Work first, eat later" was his motto. He didn't want to miss anyone who entered his store. Within an hour, tens of black hands would be stretched out with their orders. He smiled at all of them. "Patience, patience, everyone. Things will happen as God wills." Meanwhile, he'd find the time to wink at a beautiful woman or pinch a young girl's breast. He might even take delight in flirting with an old woman. He brought all the goods his clients requested and prepared their orders one by one. A kilo of rice for Abraham, a kilo of flour for Neruto, a kilo of sugar: each got what he or she needed.

The Armenian who owned the well-equipped modern store on the outskirts of the quarter wondered why he and his clerks never got to serve the large crowds that frequented Abdou Sa'id's shop.

"That Yemeni is a devil."

"He's wicked."

"By God, how does he do it?"

Abdou Sa'id always knew how much each of his customers should pay. The Armenian was astounded when he heard that the Yemeni had never been to school a day in his life.

"But how can he keep track of his accounts?"

"That cursed man is a genius!"

If the Armenian were ever to see Abdou Sa'id in the evening after he had received a letter from his village, if he were ever to watch as Abdou spent hours trying to decipher what was written in it or observe him as he held the pen, scribbling illegible letters, he would have been astonished. Abdou Sa'id, despite the difficulty, would reread his letter ten times and then methodically write his reply.

"The wicked soul makes a lot of money."

"But where does it all go?"

"Yes, it's strange. If I had as many customers as he does, I'd be a millionaire. "

"There's got to be a secret behind that man!"

"Ha! You want to pry a secret out of a Yemeni? It would be easier to pry the truth out of the devil!"

"He doesn't eat."

"He's always cooking some kind of stew."

"He's been wearing the same clothes for ten years."

"Do you think he's ever had a bath? Has he ever eaten turkey?"

But the Armenian's questions went unanswered. Abdou Sa'id didn't hear them, and if he did, he just smiled and ignored them. He opened his store at six in the morning and closed it at nine at night. For lunch, he might eat a piece of meat or some stew and bread and tea, and afterward one might find him chewing qat, as did all the Yemenis living in Marqatah and the other neighborhoods in Addis Ababa.

When he chewed qat, his customers saw mysterious things in his dazed eyes, a smile hidden in the mist of faraway dreams. But this did not prevent him from answering a customer's order and smiling, always smiling, at them all. "What is he thinking at this moment?"

"Only the devil knows."

❧ ❧ ❧

They said a lot of things about him. He had become a part of the history of the quarter. He never left, even for a day. Even on religious holidays, he wouldn't leave until ten in the morning and only after giving his customers all they required. Then he would go to visit some friends and villagers in Marqatah neighborhood, where he would have lunch and spend the day, always returning before sunset. In many instances, his evening meal would consist of only the wad of qat that stayed in his mouth while he waited on his customers.

They also said he had left behind his wife and children ten years ago and that he cried whenever he received letters from them, but no one ever saw him crying.

Abdou Sa'id could have been forty years old or perhaps thirty-five, but his age didn't seem to matter. What mattered, what people—especially the women—talked about most, was that he was a real man.

Some used to say to the envious Armenian, "Oh Subhi, if you want to attract customers like the Yemeni, you've got to please the women."

His story had begun long ago, when his beloved died, but other women followed, all of them repeating one thing: "Oh! If only you knew how much of a man he is."

"He never has enough."

If the woman was a prostitute, she would be more frank: "Listen, I've never been with a man like him in my life. I almost died of joy. How passionate, how sensual he is!"

So it was little wonder that most of his customers were women. Every one who heard about his prodigious skills wished to taste him. And though a woman might not sleep with him a second time, she would remain his customer. There was something about him that drew women to him. He was a gentle man. He flirted with them all, sometimes lasciviously, and teased them with eyes filled with confidence. Despite his huge physique, he had a baby face, smooth and supple. It looked quite handsome atop his giant body. Women often said, "Oh, my baby, don't you want to lie at my breast?" or "I wish I had a child who looked just like you."

And he'd answer, "I'd be happy if you took me with you." Or, "Oh! I'd like to, but your breasts are dried up."

Then they would laugh together like children.

"Oh, but what a shy little boy you are."

"Yes," he'd say. "But you don't know me yet."

All the children loved him too, and people said he was the father of many of them, especially those who were born white, even though their mothers were black. In the quarter, however, and in a city like Addis Ababa, there was a lot of gossip but only a little truth.

When the subject of paternity was broached with Abdou, he would say, "Why do you say I'm their father? Aren't there any other white Yemenis here?" But he added, "What you say might be true. Only God knows." And his smile grew, as did their mothers' stomachs. None of the women asked for anything, though. They only said he was the father of their children to tease him. But he loved them all and gave them caramels and lumps of sugar.

As much as he loved the children of the quarter, he loved their mothers more. He never rejected any woman who came to him. No one knew whether he himself went after them or whether they pursued him, but it was rumored that he spent a good deal of time in those elegant villas with their lush, green gardens.

They said he even made love to a fifty-year-old woman.

"Hey, listen," he remarked. "Women are all alike. They all have the same thing." But he hesitated, they said, when the matter concerned a virgin.

There was a girl who was six years old when Abdou Sa'id moved to the quarter and opened his shop. She grew up hearing the rumors about him, and as the years passed, the desire to give herself to Abdou Sa'id bloomed inside her. She imagined him as her knight, a giant on a horse with a spear in his hand, piercing the body of some terrible mythical beast, like the one in the painting of St. George that hung above her mother's bed. Her mother used to kneel before that picture and another one of a beautiful, olive-skinned woman, whose face radiated light and who held a smiling, olive-skinned child. The girl used to think that her mother was kneeling to Abdou Sa'id, for she often heard her mother talk lovingly and admiringly about him, and they went to his store many times. In fact, when she got older, she insisted that her mother send her instead of going herself.

She used to stand for hours in front of Abdou Sa'id, measuring his enormous body and childlike face, his deep eyes like those of the knight hanging in her mother's room. Her dreams were fed by what people said about him, particularly by the women who said frankly that they had "known" him.

At fifteen, she finally went to him. It was night time; a full moon hung in the sky, blurred around the edges after a light rain. Wind rattled the trees. She shivered. She had prepared herself for years for this moment, but she wanted to know, what would happen?

He greeted her as usual, "Hello, Ta'atto, what do you want?"

"Oh, nothing really, I've just come for... Oh!"

He looked at her with a wide smile as she continued to stutter incoherently.

She said, "Oh, I've forgotten, damn the devil. St. George help me."

He stood behind the counter, looking at her with his same fixed smile, with the calm, implacable gaze of a man who has all the time in the world. She felt ready to explode. Why didn't he move? And wipe that stupid smile off his face? For the first time she hated his smile. She looked feverishly at his gigantic body, her eyes lost in his.

Then he understood. He saw her heaving chest and her breasts, like two pomegranates about to explode through her old dress. Her full lips parted to show her white teeth, and he understood everything. He stopped smiling.

Beside the door was a pallet of empty sacks beside ones filled with flour, sugar, and rice. She watched him close the door quietly, then felt herself picked up, aware of his arms around her, and suddenly there she lay on those empty sacks. She fell asleep there, and it was the first time that any woman slept in the store. The next morning, she slipped out the back door, satisfaction creasing her lips into an indelible smile.

People saw that big smile, all that joy. They saw that Abdou Sa'id was happy, too. Someone might have seen a bloodstain on a sack somewhere, but no one would ask. They might not even know to ask the question, and if they did, it wouldn't matter.

Ta'atto became Abdou's mistress. Later, after her mother died, she and her household became frequent customers of Abdou Sa'id's store. Someone might have seen her in the dark, visiting him, but none could say for sure whether she was ever in Abdou's bed.

Many women had lain upon those empty sacks. The men in the quarter used to joke about it. They would say they often saw Abdou Sa'id stand outside in the morning, no matter how cold the courtyard was, and pour a bucket of water over himself. Some said he was washing himself after spending the night with a woman.

But now no one saw him taking showers. Some of the wicked ones thought that Abdou Sa'id did not like women anymore, that he had stopped sleeping around. So they got together one day and watched his store. At midnight, they saw a woman jump the fence and enter the store through the back. In the morning, Abdou Sa'id did not take a shower, but he performed ablutions and prayed over a rectangular stone in the yard.

No one knew how Abdou Sa'id had arrived in Addis Ababa or in Sodset Kilo in particular. One sunny morning, they saw him walking past, a tall stranger. The next thing they knew, he was moving in his goods and opening his store, a prayer on his lips as he worked. But where had he come from?

Some said that he had worked for the Italian army. When they expelled the army from Ethiopia, they said, Abdou Sa'id had wandered to Addis Ababa. Others said he could not have worked with the Italians, for he did not seem to know even a word of Italian, and anyone who had spent time with the Italians would speak some of the language in order to show off. They said that he had killed an Italian soldier and stolen the man's belongings, including a military blanket and overcoat. For the first few years, they said they saw these in his possession. Later they were found in the quarter, torn to pieces. Abdou also had a teapot that looked like the military teapots. Even the tin cup he used for tea was the kind only the army used, they argued.

A third group said no, no, despite his immense size, he couldn't even kill a chicken, so how could he kill a man? He didn't have the look of a killer. He had been working in Addis for a long time and had never stolen anything. If he had ever killed to steal, they reasoned, he would steal now, too. No, my dear gentlemen, they said, perhaps he earned his money working as a guard in a camel caravan. You know that caravans used to carry goods from the coast to the interior across the desert? The Dinka jungle tribes, who respect no one, would loot and steal during the war; they would attack caravans. Abdou Sa'id is a courageous man and a giant, they said. Perhaps he worked in one of those caravans. It makes sense, especially since the owners of those caravans are Yemenis, and they carry Yemeni goods. Yes, they concluded, he must have earned his money honorably, with hard work, just as he does now.

Only Abdou knew the real story and he told it to no one, not even to those women to whom he gave pleasure. He confided in no one. He even kept his sighs of pleasure to himself, behind closed lips.

Once or twice, he mentioned having been in Eritrea on the coast, but that didn't change a thing. Did his presence in there mean that he had served in the Italian army? During and after the invasion, the coasts of Eritrea had received hundreds of Yemenis, pushed from the poor coast of their country. Even Abdou Sa'id himself forgot whether he'd traveled on a dhow, boat, or a ship with torn canvas. To him, that was ancient history.

ও ও ও

But who really was Abdou Sa'id? As a boy, he had been a shepherd. He used to drink only goat's milk, which he milked secretly in the cool mountain breeze. Perhaps he ate some fruit that grew on village trees or dates that grew in the valley or bananas that he stole from a garden near the valley.

Abdou Sa'id's treasured memories were of that valley, the trees ripe with fruit, goats lowing. These were the things he remembered when he chewed leaves of qat and a far-off expression came into his eyes.

His father was a simple peasant who owned several terraced fields on the mountainside and a two-story house he had inherited through a long chain of ancestors. Abdou did not remember his mother. She had died when an epidemic struck the village, an epidemic whose name and color he had forgotten. The village had faced many such epidemics.

When he wasn't shepherding, he used to go with his father to farm the terraces on the mountainside. He helped plant seeds, pull weeds, and bring in the harvest. He still remembered the bread his grandmother used to make, spiced with fenugreek seeds, how delicious the bread was with fenugreek pudding or sometimes with porridge with yogurt and ghee in it. Those were the days.

His grandmother had died like his mother, after being sick for days. He still remembered the sound of death rattling in her throat as she lay in a corner of her room, saying, "Son, I'll get over this quickly and be well again soon." But that wasn't to be. She died without saying a word, her throat constricted. He was asleep by her side; when he awoke in the morning he felt her bony hands digging into his ribs. He had said to her, unwittingly, "Grandma, Grandma…you're hurting me."

When Abdou Sa'id was fifteen years old, he married. All he knew was that he went to the market and bought two goats, some food and clothes, and returned to the village to sit in a corner of the house. It was the same corner in which his grandmother had died and his mother before that. Next to him sat a very young girl. His wife. Three days later, she went with him to the terraced fields. At noon, she brought him bread and a plate of fenugreek. Sometimes instead of the fenugreek she would bring him dried meat.

But why did he leave his village? Perhaps Abdou Sa'id would have spent the rest of his life there. He worked during the day and chewed qat in the afternoon. He prayed from sunset to evening in the mosque.

But something new happened in the village. A family member who had emigrated sent money to Abdou's father with instructions to build him a new house. Immediately, his father began to build a three-story residence for the man. It was a lavish home, with white-painted walls and wide windows. It was like a white flourish on a black pot, the most beautiful house in the village.

Abdou was working one day with his wife, when he heard some women whispering: "Oh! Saleh Sa'id will be back this year."

"What will he think when he sees his new house?"

"He'll be back with pockets filled with money."

"His wife is so happy!"

"I wish I were his wife."

"Why don't you say you wish your husband was like him?"

The dialogue continued and his own wife joined in: "Do you know he sent silk dresses from overseas?"

"Yes, and I heard he's going to buy some land."

"They say he's very rich."

"Yes. Whoever goes overseas comes back rich."

"Why? Is money thrown in the streets there?"

Their words were like a dagger piercing his heart. He saw his young child playing in the dirt, half-naked. He felt the fenugreek burning his mouth, the loaf of bread changed into dirt as the women spoke in their sharp voices.

One day, as he was returning from the market, he spotted some women waiting by the road. They had laid their bits of wood down on a stone wall, resting after gathering firewood. He overheard them say, "Look at that house; doesn't it look like a house from paradise?"

"Yes, it's so white and beautiful."

One of them—young and attractive—said, "Who is the lucky owner of this house?"

Another laughed. "Who is his wife?"

Days later, the owner of the house arrived. It was an occasion in the village; everyone went to see him, the children leading the way. Abdou's son came back, carrying a handful of dates. He showed them to his father and said, "Look, Baba, he gave these to me." As he nibbled at them, he added, "Why don't you emigrate and bring me something like this?"

Abdou Sa'id felt that same sharp pain in his heart. He turned to his father and announced, "Father, I must emigrate."

"What about our land, Abdou?"

"You can take care of it."

"But I'm getting old."

"My wife will help you. I'll work there and send you money to hire men to help." His father wanted him to stay, but he wanted him to emigrate, too. He was unable to decide. But Abdou Sa'id made up his own mind.

"Father, I'm waiting for your blessing."

"If you insist, I'll pray for you. May God take care of you, help you, and bring you success."

And one morning, Abdou Sa'id simply left, just as many before and after him had left the village.

ﻉ ﻉ ﻉ

Now, twelve years later, he knew very little about home, except for what was revealed in the letters he received two or three times a year. Still, he was happy despite the long periods of waiting. In his heart, he lived not in Sodset Kilo, but in his faraway village in Yemen.

One day, Abdou Sa'id received a letter from home. Included were several pictures of his new house, a tall, three-story structure with wide windows that had been specially made in the town and carried to the village.

The new house was the village's bride, the letter said; it could be seen from a distance, it was so beautiful. Tears streamed down Abdou Saʿid's face, but he laughed to himself as he read the section in his son's letter: "They all like our house, some would even like to build one like it." His son's handwriting was beautiful, , exactly like the mosque teacher's handwriting he used to envy. His son had become a man, and now he had a son of his own. Abdou Saʿid felt the distance in time and miles that separated him from his home. He had become a grandfather and the owner of one of the most beautiful houses in the village. Moreover, he owned several plots of land, including the garden bordering the valley under the mountain, where he used to steal bananas as a young shepherd boy. His son, whom he had left at eight years old, now owned a store in town. In his letter, he said, "The income from the store is enough to meet our needs; we could manage if you wanted to come home and end your migration."

While the residents of the quarter did not know where his money went, Abdou knew quite well. The next morning, Abdou's customers saw the picture of his new house hanging in the middle of the store. It was a strange sight indeed. Until then, there had been only one photo in the store: an old picture of the Ethiopian governor Haile Selassie, covered with dust.

Abdou waited on his customers, tending to their orders, all the while following their eyes, which were fixed on the photo. Deep inside, he was anxious. What would they say if they knew this was his house, his own house? What sort of feelings would possess them? Were it not for modesty, he would have shown off the photo, but he couldn't. No one knew anything about him except that he smiled and waited on them. He never disclosed anything about himself or his dreams. He remained as silent as a tomb. Sometimes he would solve their problems. For example, if a maid escaped from a villa or got kicked out, he would return her, after convincing the villa's owner to raise her salary.

But he never talked about himself. Never.

The photo hung there. Curiosity ate at the customers. The design of the house was strange; it couldn't be in Ethiopia. Finally, someone shyly asked, "Whose house is that? It's beautiful!"

Happiness filled Abdou's heart. For the first time, he added extra flour to the kilo he handed the customer. Before he answered the man, he gave him a piece of candy and said, "Take this for your little boy."

He turned to the photo; he wanted to be sure of something. "Do you really think it's beautiful?"

The man nodded and Abdou said, "Yes, it's belongs to the chief of our tribe. He's a rich and courageous man. He owns a lot of land. Do you really like it?"

Abdou laughed happily when the man replied, "Indeed, such a house could only belong to a rich tribal chief."

The day passed slowly. Abdou wanted to tell everybody that the house was his, but he feared doing so for many reasons. Perhaps they wouldn't believe him and would want to know why he said it was the shaykh's house. He decided it was enough that he knew the truth. He didn't want the others to know, especially these days when he found himself suspicious of every new customer who entered his store, especially the men. He rarely talked to them unless they initiated the conversation. He always complained that he wasn't making any profit, that actually he was losing money.

He'd found out from a maid who worked for the Armenian that the man had been gossiping about him. The maid, lying in his arms, said that she heard the Armenian tell people that Abdou Sa'id had not paid taxes to the government in years. That he earned a lot, but didn't present his accounts every year, as he should. The Armenian even mentioned that he was ready to raise the issue with the government, because Abdou, he said, bribed some civil servants so that they wouldn't ask for taxes. Abdou was afraid he might really do it. If he said the house was his and that he owned land, it would mean that he had smuggled all his earnings to Yemen. If the government took the matter into consideration, he would lose everything, even his freedom.

So his happiness was mixed with a strange type of anxiety. He gave the matter a great deal of thought and was now moving toward a new idea. He worked quietly and was silent, not letting even those closest to him know what he planned.

In the evening, he closed his store. He went to buy some supplies, but did not pay as usual. He told the merchants he would pay later. He then went to the *hammam* and, though it was not yet the end of the month, he took a bath.

When he returned to the store and began to work, the residents of the quarter saw him in his new suit, the one he wore only on special occasions. He told them he hadn't had time to change. As soon as he closed the store, he shaved his beard, ate what remained of his lunch, and turned off the lights. It was past ten when he left the store, trying to take care, as much as he could, that no one saw him. In his pocket he carried a sharp knife for self-defense. He walked through quiet streets. It was springtime. Big green trees, their leaves fluttering in the breeze, brought back memories from his village. The sky was dark except for small shining stars, which disappeared behind dark clouds. .

He walked through the familiar streets. His destination was a house close to his store, but he had to take a circuitous route so no one would spot him. He walked and thought about his carefully crafted plan. His mind was occupied with thoughts of seeing his son, his land, and his new house. He did not think of his wife much. He hardly thought of her, rarely prayed for her, other than to be patient, to work on the land, to rear the children. He remembered her as he had left her, twenty-two years old, young, quiet, a simple expression on her innocent face. He sometimes smiled as he struggled to imagine her now, a woman in her thirties. Most of the time, he failed; her face was completely erased from his mind. When he succeeded, her face blended with those of ten other women he had encountered in Addis Ababa. This angered him. He did not want to compare his wife to these other women. From his perspective, she was a different type, "pure," like his country.

Abdou reached the house. He found the back door open and walked through a garden rich with the fragrance of many flowers. He stood by a rose bush, wanting to pick a rose, but he stopped when he saw light shining from one of the windows. He opened the back door of the villa and ascended the steps, knowing exactly how many there were. He rapped lightly at a door on the second floor. Seconds later, it opened. In the middle of the room stood a woman in her forties. She was black, with wide eyes and a small, delicate face. She smiled and said, "I bet you've circled the whole area."

He murmured silently.

She peered at him, seeing in his expression a strange sadness. "What's happened," she asked, "what's the matter with you?"

"Oh, nothing. I'm just tired."

She went into an interior room. He followed. She turned off the lights in the hallway. "Of course you're tired," she said, as she entered the elegant bedroom with its wide bed. "You're like a dog who can't see a piece of meat without devouring it. Why shouldn't you be tired?"

"Who told you this nonsense?"

"I hear everything," she said, smiling. "You know that."

He moved toward her and pulled her close.

She sighed with pleasure and reached up to kiss him: "Don't you know he went to Asmara and won't be back for a month? Aren't we lucky? We could meet every day, couldn't we?"

He did not answer. His hands began to touch her body, arousing a demonic lust inside him. He felt her shiver and carried her to the bed. Moments later, hot sweat covered her legs. She moaned.

"Please, they might be listening."

She pinched his cheeks affectionately and said, "You fool, I gave them the rest of the day off. There's no one here but me and you. I want to keep you until tomorrow."

He felt her sweat, and the devil re-entered his body. It was one o'clock. She was overcome with pleasure. They were naked on a bed covered in silk. The smell of perfume mixed with her sweat filled his head. She buried her face under his arm, in his thick chest hair, breathing his fragrance and the cheap soap he had washed with that day.

"Ooh! What a delicious animal you are."

She kissed everything that encountered her lips.

"Ahh! I'm thirsty, I want a drink."

She stood up from the bed, naked. Although he knew the details of her black body well, he avoided looking at her directly. Still, he saw the sweat glistening on her ebony skin and her pendulous breasts. She left the room, returning a moment later with a bottle of cold whiskey. She poured a glass and offered it to him.

He looked at her, alarmed, and murmured, "God forbid, God forbid. God protect us from its evils."

"What's wrong? Why won't you pick up your glass?"

"I don't drink. I don't even want to see alcohol. May God protect us from its evils!"

She giggled and fell down laughing by his side on the bed. Sarcastically, she said, "Poor thing, you don't drink. Why not?"

"You know it's forbidden."

"Forbidden?" she asked, surprised.

"Of course it's forbidden. That's what our religion says. You know we don't drink."

She tried to force him to take the glass, saying, "Take it. Give up this nonsense."

He got up from her bed and began putting on his clothes, saying, "I won't drink, even if I were to be chopped to pieces. Do you want me to go against my religion?"

She saw that he was serious. "But…but you sleep with women. Isn't that forbidden?"

He looked at her, worried, and continued to draw on his clothes as she stood there, drinking and looking back at him.

"What we were doing just now, isn't it forbidden, too?" she repeated. "Is alcohol more forbidden than that? Why don't you answer that you're an animal with no heart and no taste. All you want is to screw like a dog."

"I'm going back to the store."

She watched him closely, "Are you sure?"

He said, "I'm not drinking, no matter what you do."

She stood in front of him, naked, sweat shining over her body, her full breasts erect as if challenging him.

"What do you think?"

She reached out her arms to clasp his wide shoulders, stood on her toes, and looked at him, her eyes smoldering.

He closed his eyes and murmured: "God forgive us, and protect us. Oh, God, You know what is hidden inside the hearts of men."

He went back to the bed. His clothes were scattered to different parts of the room. It was unbearably hot, and he was forced to kick off the covers.

"What time will you come tomorrow?" she asked. "I'll wait for you. You know everything we do is forbidden, but no one can stop us from doing it. Isn't that so? You also know that it is not forbidden if what we want is to our benefit. Anything which benefits us cannot be forbidden. You're silent. Say something my love, my strong man."

"Oh! You know that I haven't paid any taxes for years. You've helped me a lot. But now, I've learned that that wicked Armenian wants to expose me. You know I am a poor man. I work hard to earn every cent; will you talk to your husband for me? He is a high-ranking civil servant, he could manage my case."

They lay on the bed and looked at each other for a few moments, then departed back into their own thoughts.

"Yes, yes, and this isn't forbidden in your opinion, since it's for our good as long as you're staying with me. Isn't that right? You don't agree with me in words, but in your actions you prove my theory. You look to me as a person, as an individual. This is selfishness, but I'll help you. For I want our happiness and…" She fell silent and studied him. A sad smile appeared on her face. "All you do with me may be merely a passing pleasure, so I'm seeking only my own happiness, my own pleasure." She looked at him with disdain: "Do you know what happiness is?"

He looked dumbly at her, and thought as he murmured, "Happiness!"

A scene flashed before his eyes, of the new house in the village, the new land; then he returned to the strange woman.

"You don't know the agony of these nights. You're an animal…" She did not wait for his response. "No, you don't know what it is. Happiness is not something tangible. It's a feeling. A delicious feeling. We feel it when we make love; we search for it for years and might find it only for a moment, but it's worth all the years of sadness. You don't know what it's like for a woman to live with a husband who sleeps by her side like a rotten corpse, a husband made of bones. When he kisses her, she feels his rotten breath, suffocating her. You can't know the suffering of those nights. You're an animal. Nothing concerns you, not even a woman in your arms. You quench your thirst. You live in a mirage, my friend, a mirage."

Abdou's thoughts were far away. He heard her voice as if it were coming from the bottom of a deep well. She would help him so that he would not have to pay taxes this year, either. This meant his plan was moving toward success. How he would laugh at that Armenian!

A tight cloud of gloom descended upon him. Soon he would leave the entire quarter to the Armenian. And that was what the Armenian had wanted for years. Oh! Would he be able to best the Armenian before he finally left? If so, how?

"We'll continue because we need each other," said the woman, her voice barely penetrating his thoughts. "But then, what's the point if it's merely for need; when can we live the way we wish?"

Abdou thought about a time when he could finally live as he wished. What a beautiful dream come true: to pray every morning on the roof of his new house so that the village people could see him, to go to the garden to pick from his fruit. Just to prove his authority, he would chase out the children and prevent the women from resting in the shade of his garden when they returned from gathering wood.

People would say, "Whose house is this?"

"Oh! What a great house!"

Then he would finally hear the answers he had dreamed of for years on those cold winter nights as the moon dreamed of spring. "This house, the garden, and those terraced fields on the mountain all belong to Abdou Sa'id."

"Yes! And not only does he own that, he also owns a large store in town, which is managed by his son. "

Then people would ask, "Who is this man? Where did he come from?" He would listen to the answers with a satisfied smile on his face. They'd all say, "Oh, who doesn't know Abdou Sa'id? He owns the most beautiful house in the village!"

"What are you thinking of, my dear?" asked the woman. "Morning is getting close. Take me into your arms."

∿ ∿ ∿

Around six that evening, Ta'atto entered his store. He looked at her, surprised. He hadn't seen her in a long time, not since she became a prostitute in the quarter with many lovers and clients.

"Good evening," she said. " Did I startle you?" She looked at him with big beautiful eyes and a quiet smile filling her small black face. "Or did you forget that young girl you made into a woman in a matter of minutes?"

She was a beautiful, mature woman now, full of passion; she could seduce any man who came near her. She was quiet. Abdou continued to chew some small leaves of qat. He looked at her without answering.

"What a strange man. You chew qat leaves and then on the twigs. How this reminds me of the breasts of all those you spit out after sucking their youth."

"How is it even you would say such a thing?" he replied, devouring her with his eyes. "What brings you here?"

She smiled and said, "Don't worry; I didn't come to tell you you've become a father of another child. It's enough that so many of the children in this quarter are yours. What a heart of stone you have! How can a human being leave his sons when he knows damn well they're his?"

She moved toward the counter. "I've come to tell you that Fatimah died yesterday." When he still made no reply, she added, "When she died, she left a young boy. Your son. He's alone, doesn't belong to anyone. Fatimah had no family, and I gave it a lot of thought before coming to you. I already know that you're a worthless person, but maybe deep inside you the instinct of fatherhood might be born. He's your son, Abdou. You've got to do something for him. You must!"

Abdou's face expressed many things, and he felt the qat constrict his throat. He had seen the boy several times, playing with the other kids in the quarter; the child even looked like him. Then he remembered the proverb, "A bastard always looks like his father." He was white like Abdou, with the same innocent baby face, though he had his mother's kinky hair and full Negroid lips. But what could he do? He had decided to leave everything and go back home, to escape to his new house, to his land, which he had bought with years of hard work. To see his son, yes, his real son, his lawful son, but this, oh God, what was to be done? He could not love this son.

The girl was waiting for his answer. What should he tell her?

He had never before faced a problem like this. He was the one who solved other people's problems. Goddamn the dirty animal who brought this upon him. Why did this woman have to give birth when she knew that her son would be a bastard? He repeated the word in his head. What would people say when they knew that the child was his son, no, that he was his *bastard* son? What would his wife say, she who prayed and waited patiently for his return? What would he say to his son, who had grown into an important man? He must get rid of this matter…he must.

"So, what do you say?" Ta'atto asked. "What will you do?"

He was silent and hesitant. Oh, Abdou, he thought. Think of something to tell her!

Impatiently, she said, "Oh, Abdou. I thought you were a good man at heart. Now I don't know what you are, but I'll never forget you. I love you. I never said that to you, and I don't like to say it, but what can I do? You were the dream of my virginity. How badly I wanted you as my man. I gave you everything and asked for nothing in return. I was courageous. Will you for once be courageous? It's you who can save this child; you're his father. Remember his mother, how kind she was, may God bless her soul. She spoke about you all the time." Ta'atto sighed sadly; tears ran down her beautiful cheeks.

Abdou hesitated, but then after a silence said, "What do you want me to do? If I take him in, all the other women will come and throw their children at me. I work very hard for my living, to earn a few coins. By God, how can you ask me to join a bastard to my name? Who knows if he's even mine? I can't do anything for you."

He paced slowly in the store, his face strained and ugly.

"I know how despicable you are," said Ta'atto. "But I thought you might have mercy on the child!"

He shook his head in sorrow. "Child? What child? It's a bastard you're talking about. You know if he were a legal son, the matter would be altogether different. Do you want to ruin me? I'm sure all the women with bastards in the quarter would bring their children saying, 'He's their father.' I'm not stupid."

"But you really *are* their father. The father of many children. Or have you forgotten? Did you forget me, the girl you made into a woman on the empty flour sacks in this corner? How I hate the rotten smell of your store now, but when I was a stupid child I thought it was as sweet as perfume. I still remember everything, Abdou, and, unfortunately, I was happy, very happy with you. But now it's clear to me that though everybody knows that you are 'a man,' you don't possess a man's heart. You are a heartless animal."

As she spoke, tears ran down her face. He looked at her. Inside him, the animal stirred. She was much more beautiful now than she had been as a child. He had never seen a woman cry in front of him; how beautiful they were when they shed tears. How beautiful was Ta'atto now. He desired her and wanted to take her.

His eyes opened wide. "I don't have a heart, huh? If only you knew how much I suffer, how I kill myself working. I own an honest business. I would like to live in my home again. I would like to die after I've done good things for my son and wife. No, Ta'atto, you know nothing. First I'll go to Mekkah and perform the Hajj. All my sins will be forgiven. Then I'll return to my village. There, I'll stay in the mosque, worshipping God day and night. God commands us, Ta'atto, to work as hard as we can, to work for our children, our legal children. But I have only one son. God created those others, and He will take care of them. Why would He create bastards if He didn't plan to take care of them? It's not me but God who's responsible. Oh, Ta'atto, you're so beautiful, so very beautiful when you cry."

Ta'atto replied, "Have mercy on this child; he has no one else. The others have mothers. They don't need you; each has her own work. No one wants anything from this miserable store of yours."

Abdou stared at her blankly.

"Be human for once!"

Abdou closed the door of the store and said, "Listen, let's think about this. I can't just accept out of the blue that I've got a son. You know that."

He came closer to her. She thought that he wanted to say other things; through her tears she saw him approach. He put his hands on her shoulders and kissed her firmly. She felt his heat, and the smell of the store entered her nostrils from the thick hair on his chest. Memories of their past flooded her mind. But Fatimah had died only yesterday. She wiped her tears, pulled away angrily from him and said, "There are thousands of stupid drunks with hearts of gold. There are poor men who don't own a single franc but who will sell themselves for their children to live, even if those children are bastards. But you"—as he tried to approach her again, she finished—"you are an ass."

She slapped Abdou's face violently, cursing him, "Dog…filthy…ass. I'll show you what I'll do. I'll expose you for what you are, you animal."

When he pulled himself together, he was alone in the store. Traces of her perfume lingered, making the animal inside him weep. He went into the back, still feeling the sting of her blows. Abdou, a tribal man, had just been slapped by a woman. He allowed no one to humiliate him, and here a prostitute and a bastard had done just that. This woman, whose body all men knew, had rejected him. He had never been refused by a woman before. The whore! Moments before, she had told him she loved him. But she was wicked, he knew. She wanted to blackmail him and saddle him with the bastard. Oh, he would take his revenge on her. She had come to cheat him; she thought he was stupid. What a bitch. Her job was to cheat men, but he wasn't like the others. He was tribal. He would drink her blood.

He was shaken from his reverie by the entrance of a customer who said, "I need some cigarettes and matches."

Without thinking, Abdou answered, "I'm all out."

But the man thought Abdou had forgotten that he had cigarettes, and said, "The cigarettes are right there. What's wrong with you today?"

"I tell you I'm all out!" he shouted at the man.

"But…"

"Didn't you hear me? I don't want to sell anything. I'm free to do as I please. Now get out of my store."

The man left, murmuring, "Abdou is going crazy."

The man met another customer and they exchanged a long whisper as they looked in Abdou's direction. The man's face was red and his lips moved continuously, as if he was muttering imprecations. They saw him shake his fist angrily in the air.

"He's lost his mind."

"I thought he lost it a long time ago."

"He wouldn't be able to live like this if he weren't crazy."

"We've got to warn people."

"Did you see him shouting at me? He could've killed me. The poor fool. If we knew his family, we could ask them to take him to the hospital."

Abdou was immersed in his dream of vengeance, mentally threatening the woman who had awakened his tribal urges, steeped in his knowledge that a man humiliated by a woman can only cleanse himself with blood!

ﻉ   ﻉ   ﻉ

Ta'atto talked fervently. Sayyid Amin listened, occasionally murmuring to himself. Tears ran down her cheeks, and the sayyid kindly said, "Don't worry, my child. God will fix matters!"

"Please, my master, I know I'm a Christian, that your God is not mine, but we're all human. I can't take care of this child on my own; you know I work as a sinner. But what can I do? I've got to make a living. Tomorrow, I'll lose my youth and no one will even look at me anymore, so I must save some money for that time. I know none of the men who frequent my house today will take me as his wife, but…"

She looked at him, her tears still running hotly. He murmured, his beads falling in musical harmony. She was about to kiss his hand, but he quickly pulled it away. She said, "Forgive me for bothering you, but I had to do this. Will you forgive me, my father? You're the only person who can convince him."

Sayyid Amin was in his fifties, with a thick beard and a face that seemed to be illuminated by an inner light. There was a black mark on his forehead from prostrating in prayer. He was a good man who received anyone with a problem, and was frequented by Muslims and Christians alike.

Sayyid Amin promised to help as much as he could, playing with his beads as he spoke. "Don't worry, my girl. God is omnipresent and He is kindest to humans. He will not forget His creatures. Go home. Everything will be taken care of. Wipe your tears and go."

Ta'atto hadn't attended church since she was a child, and now she wanted to confess all her sins to the man with the radiant face who sat before her. She wanted to tell him how much she loved Abdou Sa'id. To her, the sayyid represented father, priest, and divine messenger; she thought he could say words to his Lord to erase her sins. She looked at him, hope shining in her eyes.

"Oh! Father, pray to your kind Lord to have mercy upon me."

The shaikh smiled. "God accepts your prayers. If you really, sincerely, want to repent, do good and abandon evil. God is forgiving and kind. Don't tell anyone you talked to me concerning this matter. God will inspire me; don't forget this. Now leave me alone to think."

Ta'atto left with a hope growing inside her that God would forgive her many sins. He was her only hope. After all weren't they all sons and daughters of Adam and Eve? She knew that she was sinning. But what could she do? Her alternative was to die of hunger. God would have to wait until her house was empty of customers; yes, she had to wait until no one desired her anymore. By then she would have saved some money and she would be ready for God.

The shaikh said that God was forgiving and kind. God knew what her problem was; indeed it was He who planned this path for her. As she walked, she looked up at the sky, praying and pleading and filled with a hope that grew and grew. Spring was embracing Addis Ababa, transforming it into a beautiful garden.

۩ ۩ ۩

Sayyid Amin called his son and ordered him to go to Hajji Abdul Latif and tell him that the sayyid wanted to see him right away. His son went quickly.

The sayyid felt that before him now lay the life of a child he had to save from destruction. Sayyid Amin himself had left Yemen when he was twenty years old and entered the religious school of Jabala, where he mastered the religious sciences. He had found Ethiopia a wide-open place, full of followers. When he reached forty-years-old, he secluded himself inside his big house, staying in his room, which was partitioned into two areas. One was a private section no one entered, not even his wife, where he spent half of each month alone. Food was offered to him through a small window. He stayed there, praying. His followers claimed that angels frequently visited his room and talked to him. They had heard a soft kind voice conversing with the sayyid about religious matters.

He hadn't left his home for the last ten years. No one knew how he showered or answered his call to nature. They always saw him with a clean, white face, radiant with blessings. Where and how did he make his living? His followers said that each month the angels carried to his family all that they needed. The truth was that at the beginning of each month someone sent all they needed. The sayyid always said, "All of this is blessings from God. His kindness is great!"

Whenever the sayyid came out from his seclusion, he seemed happier and would smile more and say mysterious things. He designated the second half of the month to meet with people and solve their problems, advising them and teaching them on different religious matters.

Despite his seclusion, he was well known in Addis Ababa. His counsel was particularly sought after during the feast days, and no one could count the number of gifts he received during these occasions.

The sayyid did not go to the local mosque for the Friday prayer, and in Addis Ababa it was known that no sounds could be heard from his private internal alcove either. It was rumored that he attended Friday prayers at three mosques each month: at the Aqsa mosque in Jerusalem, from which the Prophet was taken on his nocturnal ascent to heaven, twice in Mekkah, and another time in Medina.

But how did he get there? Some said that angels carried him, that like the angels he was dressed in white clothes, and that they flew him there so he could say his Friday prayers. Some said that he rode the Prophet's mythical

41

horse, al-Burak. They said the horse came and carried the sayyid to the mosque. Despite the different reports, all agreed that the sayyid prayed at those mosques in person.

Some of the followers—many of them young men—doubted this, so they watched him enter his alcove. Their reports differed, too. It was said that no sound was heard in the niche, as if there was no one inside. No one brought food. Others said they heard low quiet voices, which they explained as whispers of angels that came to take the sayyid to Jerusalem. The essential thing they agreed on was that the sayyid was more than a mere holy man; he was a pure spirit.

Hajji Abdul Latif entered and respectfully kissed the sayyid's hand, then quietly sat. He was a short man with a full body and a small beard. He was forty-five, one of the rich Yemenis of Addis Ababa who were leaders of the community. He had played a role in the 1948 revolution, for he was one of the Yemeni liberals; until today, he still believed in that cause and offered lots of help.

He looked at the sayyid's mouth, which followed the beads as they fell. He kept silent for a while, peering at the sayyid with his own wide eyes. The hajji's face turned red several times and he thought, *What's going on? Why is he looking at me like that? What does he want?* Before he could continue on in this vein, the sayyid said, "Yes, Hajji, you've got the right to ask why I asked you to come here today. But it's not what you might think; it's for something else."

The hajji knew that the sayyid sometimes read what was in a person's mind. He blamed himself for doubting the cause of his call, but the sayyid said, "Don't blame yourself, for God knows what secrets lurk in the hearts of men. I've called you to discuss a matter that is important to God and His true religion."

Signs of curiosity appeared on Hajji Abdul Latif's face, as the sayyid continued talking, his beads falling like autumn leaves between his fingers. "It's an important matter concerning the fate of a human being. I learned of the matter while in seclusion. I heard a sweet voice say: 'Why do you leave a Muslim in the hands of Christians? Why don't you rush to save him? If this happens while you live, what if you died? You, Sir, are responsible for God's servant.' I answered, saying, 'But Lord, how is Your poor servant to know? I was praying for You in my seclusion, seeking Your forgiveness. The voice replied, 'It's all right. I know what is in the hearts of men, but I tell you, praying alone is not enough. What's more important is saving Muslim spirits from hell. Know this: that someone named Abdou Sa'id committed the sin of fornication with a woman called Fatimah, who gave birth to a boy. I've called Fatimah to my side but she left a bastard son, born of Muslim parents, in the care of an infidel woman. Go quickly and save his soul; if you do, you'll win my blessing in Paradise.'"

The sayyid spoke in a commanding yet gentle voice. He looked piercingly at the hajji, who lowered his gaze and shook his head, saying, "How great, oh Lord, You who makes known the unknown and reveals the secrets."

"Hajji Abdul Latif, God revealed something for the benefit of humankind. I said to the sweet voice, 'You know, Lord, that Your servant loves no one but You and knows no one in this big city, for he is preoccupied with prayers.' The sweet voice answered: 'We know everything. Call our servant, Abdul Latif, and relate everything I've said to you.'"

As he listened to this, deep joy filled Hajji Abdul Latif's heart, for he believed that the Lord knew him and asked the sayyid to seek his help. "Oh, Almighty God, the greatest, oh my Lord; that means that I'm a good man, and God is satisfied with me. Oh, Lord, how great You are!"

"Don't be arrogant, Hajji Abdul Latif. The Lord only wants to examine your faith and your ability to do His will. It is a very difficult test. Victory goes only to those who pass with the Lord's forgiveness. So go right away to this man and don't say a word of what I've told you. It is our secret. Try to handle him gingerly and persuade him as much as you can."

He looked straight through the hajji and in a voice so loud it shook the hajji's heart, said, "And if you fail, God will be waiting with the results of your test." He shook his head and his fingers started counting the beads. His other hand stroked his henna-painted beard. "I envy you, oh Hajji, for this blessing. But I'm sure that God has put His trust in the right man."

Inside, the hajji felt a childlike joy. He wanted to rush outside and shout to everyone: "God has chosen me, specially, to save a human being from becoming a Christian. Listen to me! God loves me!"

But before he could rush out, the sayyid said, "I said don't get carried away. God's love does not mean that He will overlook the wrong you do, but rather that He is watching and He does not forget or neglect anything. So be alert and carry out the mission for which you've been chosen, and may you be blessed with money and children."

The hajji stood and kissed the sayyid's hand though he tried to pull away. Before the hajji disappeared, the sayyid said, "Oh, and Hajji, don't forget to help the woman who took care of this child."

Overjoyed, Abdul Latif left. He walked, oblivious to everything around him, even the dozens of people who greeted him. He walked as if he were flying. His eyes filled with tears of joy and gratitude, he looked up at the sky and thought about what he'd tell his friends tomorrow. But why tomorrow and not today? No, he chastised himself; he had to carry out his mission. He would start searching for the man, asking for him among the Yemeni community.

When he entered the store, his secretary approached him and as usual gave the hajji the account book. But the hajji looked at the secretary and smiled, saying, "Oh, my son, do this job by yourself. I've got an important mission to do, commissioned by God."

The secretary looked at him, surprised.

The hajji exclaimed, "Why do you look at me this way? Oh, you're still a young man, you've got to know God never forgets His creatures. He remembered me."

The secretary smiled, for he knew that the hajji had visited the sayyid. Later he said, "Do you want me to send anything to the sayyid?"

"May God guide you. God in His love for me gave you a good mind. Yes, quickly send perfume, frankincense, clothes…" And he mentioned many more things.

The secretary smiled as he jotted down notes. Then the hajji said, "Yes, he's a holy man, one of the greatest saints; if we had more like him, we would have liberated Yemen a long time ago. But what could we do? All the young men like you have given up their religion. God is upset with us because of you. But He won't forget His creatures."

He sat down behind his desk and dreamed of paradise.

❧ ❧ ❧

The next morning, Hajji Abdul Latif went around to the different stores of Marqatah asking about Abdou Sa'id. Finally, someone sent him to Saleh Saif's store. Hajji Abdul Latif carried out his mission with a feeling of contentment and superiority. True, he had been commissioned several times by the Liberal Party to do other great tasks. To liberate the Yemen, he had organized community meetings, raised funds, even given emotional speeches mixed with prayers, religious rhetoric, and political enthusiasm.

He entered Saleh Saif's store, a huge smile on his lips. After exchanging greetings with the proprietor, the hajji launched into his purpose: "My dear friend, I came to you on a very important matter, one that requires our cooperation, for it concerns our religion and our country."

From the moment the hajji entered the shop, Saleh Saif thought he was there to solicit another campaign donation and tried to think of ways to get rid of him. He knew the hajji was an ambitious person and wouldn't accept only a small contribution. Saleh's mind was spinning. He prayed to God to help him out of this new problem. True, he believed in the ideas of the liberals, and he had donated money and read their pamphlets. When the revolution broke out, he was enthusiastic about it; he had actually considered going back to the Yemen to begin a new life under the revolutionary government.

But the revolution had died in its infancy, years passed, and day after day Saleh Saif started to lose his faith in the new revolution and the reform of Yemeni affairs. He showed his dissatisfaction over the more frequent requests for donations. But he always gave money, and he knew now that since the hajji came personally, with this big smile on his lips, that it would be a request for a large sum. But Hajji Abdul Latif surprised him, saying, "You know that giving up the child of two Muslim parents to be raised by unbelievers makes that child an unbeliever according to Islam. Our true religion orders us to save such children. I came here to tell you that it's not a secret anymore…"

What has a child got to do with religion and homeland, Saleh thought. But he kept quiet and waited to find out what was going on.

"It appears that a man you know, Abdou Sa'id, committed the sin of fornication with a Muslim woman, who gave birth to a boy. She died, leaving her child in the hands of an ill-reputed Christian woman. So I came to you to discuss saving this small soul and bringing it back to Islam."

Saleh sighed, relieved that it wasn't a matter of new donations.

"Do you know Abdou Sa'id?" asked the hajji.

"Yes, I do."

"So let's go together and talk him into taking care of his son."

Saleh thought for a moment and then asked, "Fine, but don't you think that Abdou Sa'id will refuse to admit that the child is his? I know him. He's an upstanding man and married back in his village, with a son; he's been here for more than fourteen years. He's a good Muslim. I don't think he'll confess that he committed fornication."

The hajji laughed. "It's strange. This is not a matter of confession. You know there's not a single Yemeni in Ethiopia who hasn't known at least one woman here. Is it reasonable for a man to remain alone for years without getting close to a woman? The idiot should have been more careful, but he did it. He has no choice but to foster the child."

"It's not as simple as you think to just go tell him, 'This child is your son.'" He looked questioningly at the hajji. "But how did you learn about this? Who told you?"

The hajji smiled and was about to tell the man about how God had chosen him to fulfill this mission. But then he remembered the sayyid's warning. So he said, in a quiet but sharp voice that gave the impression he knew things by charismatic magical power, "The matter is known to God and the believers. God counts the births of His creatures, so why not a man who begot a bastard?"

46

Saleh Saif nodded, convinced: "So you think we should talk to him? I don't mind going along, especially since he'll listen to you as a leader. But how will you approach the subject with him?"

Thoughtfully, the hajji said, "God is with us, and if He wants something to be done, it will be done."

The car moved along from the Marqatah to Sodset Kilo. Both men were silent, each thinking of the proper approach to use with Abdou Sa'id. Saleh Saif knew the man well. Abdou was tight with his money; he always wore the same suit. Saleh Saif had no idea where the man's money went. Abdou rarely visited him. He didn't seem to care about Yemeni affairs or liberation.

How many times had Saleh Saif seen Abdou fold up the newspapers in his shop without even thinking to read them? He never gave donations or attended community meetings. He lived in complete isolation, visiting the Marqatah once a month to buy supplies for his store. In fact, Saleh had never visited him and wasn't even sure which street his house was on.

"Listen, does this Abdou earn a lot?" the hajji asked, his attention on the road. "How can I put it?" answered Saleh. "He must be making a lot, but no one knows where his money goes."

"Does he send money to his family?"

"He never tells me anything. He visits me on occasion but usually gets bored with our parties and leaves."

"Is he a pious man? Does he pray? Fast?"

"I believe so."

"If he is pious, then where does his money go? He must be drinking alcohol, mother of all evils, and spending all his money on it."

Saleh Saif did not answer. But he secretly smiled.

(Later the hajji's secretary commented, after hearing the hajji's opinion on alcohol: "We say that with our tongues, but in our hearts, we worship it." And he winked to those around him. "The hajji avoids accusations, but forgets to cover his breath with mint when he reviews the accounts each night.")

"Why are you quiet? If the man fornicates, it's no surprise that he also drinks alcohol, is it?"

"You yourself, Hajji…I mean we, the Yemenis, know all sorts of women; does that mean we all drink?"

But the hajji answered, "I said that about the young men who are bachelors. As for us, thanks to God, we have families and children. We have no need to commit such sins."

But Saleh was laughing inside, for he knew well Hajji Abdul Latif and his cronies. He wanted to say, "And you've never tasted alcohol, Hajji?" But he was quiet, for the car had stopped on one of Sodset Kilo's quiet streets.

The hajji shouted at one of the Ethiopian pedestrians, "Do you know where Abdou Sa'id's store is?" Of course he did. Was there anyone in this quarter who did not know Abdou's store?

The car stopped in front of the store. It was noon. A spring sun cast its rays through the leaves, etching beautiful shadows on the ground. The children playing on the street corner noticed the car stop and the hajji and Saleh climb out and head to the store. This was a new scene for the children; many days had passed since anyone had come in a car to Abdou's store, or without a car for that matter! They rushed to see the elegant clothes of the guests. One of them whispered, "How come we've never seen Abdou in clothes like theirs?"

None of them replied. Their eyes were fixed on the two men who shook hands with Abdou and greeted him with friendly smiles.

Of course, Abdou did not expect anyone to visit him in his store, least of all Hajji Abdul Latif. His heart pumped furiously when he saw the car pull up before the store and the hajji and Saleh Saif get out. He wondered why they would come to his store? When he saw the smiles on their faces, he became even more worried, wondering whether it might have something to do with donations. But the hajji had been collecting contributions for a long time, so why had he not come to him before? Even Saleh Saif, when they used to visit together, never talked about the matter. True, he used to ask Abdou to read the newspapers, and sometimes he would take the opportunity during holidays to speak about the progress in the

Yemen or to refute the claims of the government of the Imam. But he never asked Abdou for a donation. So, there must be a different reason, but what was it?

The two men stood in front of Abdou. They were baffled since there were no chairs in the store and, except for his bed and sacks of flour and rice, no place to sit. Abdou was baffled as well. Should he invite them in to sit on the bed? But the room was so dirty…and the bed was just some boxes and an old blanket.

The two men fidgeted, uncomfortably. The place was too stuffy, and had a smell they had forgotten since the days when they owned their own stores before the war, small grocery stores like this. They found it hard to believe that such stores still existed. Everything looked so unusual. The store, thought small, was filled with all sorts of goods piled in complete chaos. And the man who stood before them was an eccentric character, his black clothing dirty with oils and ghee and other things that had spilled on it.

The hajji had a long introduction in his mind, which he now tried to recollect—Quranic verses and sayings of the Prophet, prayers for the man. But all of that flew out of his mind as he stood in front of Abdou, who tried to smile.

A group of customers passed by, but they quickly walked away as they saw the guests standing with Abdou. One of them wondered, *Did they come to take him away? He's really crazy, the poor man. He lost his smile days ago. Perhaps they'll take him to a doctor.* And he left sadly, shaking his head at Abdou's fate.

The hajji, wrinkled his nose at the smell that filled his head, especially the smell of Abdou's villager's lunch, mixed with the smells of soap, ghee, oil, and other things. He said, "I've come to speak with you concerning your son."

His voice was strong and harsh. He spoke so curtly that Abdou was taken completely by surprise. He started to respond, but the hajji continued, "People know, and you've got to take your son and rear him. Isn't it forbidden to leave him for the unbelievers, to a dishonorable woman, to leave him orphaned, living a life of loss?"

When Abdou heard the words "your son," his thoughts flew to his son in Yemen, but he checked himself when he heard the last phrases. It all became clear.

Saleh Saif looked at Abdou, concerned that the hajji had launched into the subject without any preamble, though his fervor was understandable.

Eyes darted quickly about at nothing. Silence. Anxious eyes.

Abdou spoke: "So, she went to complain to you? I didn't think of that. I didn't think you'd listen to a prostitute. I thought you were a great thinker, but…"

Four eyes froze in their sockets. What did he mean?

Saleh Saif looked at the hajji. Blood boiled in his head. His face was bright red from the humiliation that tore at him, but he checked his temper.

"Fear God, man. What are you saying? We came to advise you. We came to you so that Ethiopians won't say that we leave our sons in the streets for unbelievers."

"But who told you he's my son?"

"God told me," the hajji replied, angrily.

Abdou's eyes were red. "Then let God rear him."

"What? Seek forgiveness from God! You've blasphemed. God says, 'Whoever commits a sin, he should fix it with a pious deed.' But you're making it worse."

Here Saleh Saif got involved, trying to be wiser, more rational: "Listen friends, it's nonsense to talk like this. Why don't we move outside? The breeze will help us think much more clearly. What do you say?"

He took the hajji's arm and led them all out into the street. The weather was beautiful, the sun warm.

"Listen, Abdou," said Saleh. "We're from the same country, which makes us cousins. We are all Yemenis. If something hurts one of us, it hurts us all, so we came to you. We aren't here to call each other names, but to shake hands as brothers. "

Abdou was silent.

"What concerns the hajji is that leaving the boy with the Christians would mean a Muslim soul might be led to godlessness. As Muslims, we can't let these Muslim children go to hell, can we?"

Abdou looked at him and smiled bitterly. "You couldn't find anyone else to go to? I'm the poor guy you had to talk to; why don't you go check on the others? How many of the rich ones among them have bastards? Tell me, how many?"

Saleh persisted calmly, "Only God knows the truth of what you're saying, but we heard of your case, so we came to you."

"Oh, yeah, you've heard," Abdou replied, sarcastically. "Who told you? It was that whore, wasn't it?"

Here the hajji exploded: "Don't accuse people of such things; Sayyid Amin told me."

A terrible silence engulfed them. Abdou stared at the two men in disbelief.

"Who…who…the sayyid?"

"Yes, Sayyid Amin told me."

"How did he find out about this? How?"

Both Abdou and Salah Saif wore expressions of surprise. They'd both heard a great deal about the sayyid, but didn't think he knew people's secrets.

The hajji knew he had the upper hand now. He said, "The sayyid knows many things; nothing is unknown to him."

"But why did he choose me in particular? There are many…"

The hajji interrupted: "Their turns will come."

Abdou thought, *Did Ta'atto go to the sayyid? But he doesn't meet with prostitutes; he's a pious, saintly man. Was he divinely inspired? Is that possible? That would mean God is angry with me.* Suddenly, he was gripped with a terrible fear.

"Friends—what do you think I should do?"

"It's simple, you must take your son and raise him."

"But I can't. I've decided to go back to Yemen. How can I bring a bastard with me?"

"Return to Yemen—but why?"

"Just like that, I'm going back."

The hajji laughed. "You see! He's crazy; he said he'll return to Yemen. He thinks it's paradise over there, that the Imam suddenly became a good and gentle ruler. Listen, the situation in Yemen remains as it is. No one can live there. Trust me. There's no point in returning until after the revolution."

"But I don't care about the situation. I want to go home, to farm my land and live with my wife and son. How can I take this bastard along?"

"Tell them you married again."

"What? Do you want me to lie? I can't. God alone knows if he is my son."

"Oh, man, fear God. Do you think that the sayyid and we would lie to you?"

Anxiety tore at Abdou. He didn't know how to answer them. He knew the boy was his son, but a bastard, the son of an illegal relation. How could he agree to take him in?

"Next all the women will come with their bastard children and claim that I'm their father."

The two men looked at each other. They smiled.

"When did you decide to return?" asked Saleh.

"I'll go on pilgrimage first, and at the end of the year I'll return home."

"What about the store?"

"I've started to get rid of things already."

"Have you thought it over carefully?"

"Yes, for over two years, and now you come up with this calamity."

The hajji laughed and said, "We? Who told you to sleep with all these women?"

"I'm a man."

"And this is God's judgment."

Saleh added, "And His punishment."

"Oh, yes, God only punishes the poor! But the rich..."

Saleh shook his head. "Listen, God does not differentiate between his servants. Everyone receives his punishment."

"But the poor get punished first."

"Have you lost your faith?"

Abdou was perplexed. The two men were silent, each deep in thought. The hajji had started to doubt the situation; how did Sayyid Amin know of Abdou's problem unless he got the information from the woman Abdou talked about? But that was very difficult, for he knew the sayyid receive people only rarely, and why would he receive a woman who sells herself to men?

Deep inside, he started to wonder if the sayyid had lied to him. But it was still possible he had told the truth. In either case, the hajji was happy, for God had chosen him for this mission, which seemed to be growing more troublesome. If the sayyid had lied, he would bear the consequences of that; but he—the hajji—would still receive his reward from God.

"All right, Abdou, what have you decided?"

"I don't know."

Here the hajji smiled encouragingly: "Come on, my man, it's simple. Think it over. We will be back again in a couple of days. God will not forget those who do good works. You'll be saving the life of a soul and giving him the opportunity to join the true religion, not leaving him to the care of unbelievers."

Saleh shook hands with Abdou, as did the hajji. Moments later the car disappeared at the end of the street.

Abdou stood in front of his store, thinking: *They talk about good deeds, they, the scoundrels who get involved in all sorts of scandals, and no one says anything to them...but we, the poor, they count each breath we take.*

Good deeds: if the hajji wanted to save the boy, son of a bitch, why didn't he take him in? Why did he sentence me? Goddamn lust and pleasure; who told her to get pregnant? Oh God, I seek your forgiveness, but your servant is wretched.

God created the child, and He is the great provider. If divine inspiration revealed the situation to Sayyid Amin, that means God knows about it and so will take care of him. Yes, I could be his father, God knows, and He is the forgiving and the beneficent, and He will not take a poor man with a sin. Oh God, I'll perform the hajj and repent for all my sins and will stay pious to the end of my life. Just help me out of this mess, oh God.

That night he did not sleep. He went to the villa and while they were in bed told her everything.

She smiled at him. "So they found out. What are you worried about? You can refuse, since you don't feel fatherly love toward the poor boy. If they are so intent on saving him from becoming an unbeliever, they should take care of him themselves."

She looked at the man lying by her side. Sarcastically, she said, "What kind of a man are you? You make babies for the poor. As for me, you don't know how much I want a child from you. Oh, God, if only you would give me a child!"

He paid no attention to her; the problem nagged at him. How would he be able to return to the village with a bastard? The woman said, "I wouldn't say that you're his father. I'll bring him up educated, cultured. Oh, God, if only you gave me a child! I'll sacrifice daily to the Virgin Mary and pray to St. George and light dozens of candles for him under his statue. I'll feed the poor. Oh, Virgin, give me a child!"

ى   ى   ى

The sayyid looked at Hajji Abdul Latif and shook his head. Dropping his beads to the floor, he said sharply, "So he brought destruction upon himself. He committed a sin and doesn't want to carry out God's will. Well, God will take His revenge upon him. He will be merciless. Leave him to his offense; his transgressions will accumulate, and in the end it will be like a flood. As for me, he who gives warning to a transgressor cannot be blamed."

His beard shook as he spoke. His face turned red, and the veins in his hands stood out.

"Now, Hajji, leave me alone with my Lord, to complain to Him about the gross injustices and sins of His creatures. You go to the child and save him. You, Hajji, save a Muslim soul from disbelief. God has chosen you to save him. Don't hesitate. Go now."

Before Hajji Abdul Latif could reply, the sayyid disappeared into a niche, pulling the curtain closed. The scent of frankincense filled the room.

The hajji felt the weight of the problem upon his shoulders. What would he do, faced with this *fait accompli*?

He mentally cursed Abdou Sa'id. He was about to curse the sayyid, too, but was still afraid of him. He returned, distressed, to his store. How would he add a boy he didn't even know to his extended family? All to save him from becoming an unbeliever. What had he done to deserve this? Hadn't God created this child? Shouldn't He take care of him? If God wanted to save the boy's soul, why did He put him in the hands of unbelievers?

Oh, God, he didn't know the answer. He had fallen short somehow, and now he had to extricate himself from this mess. But how? Yesterday, Abdou Sa'id had flatly refused to adopt the child, said he wasn't the father of anyone, and cursed them all, telling them not to interfere in his private life. Did the hajji now have to carry a "bastard" for the sake of a brother Muslim? Did that mean that it was now his responsibility to save the souls of every bastard born to Yemenis in Ethiopia? God damn them all. He had enough problems. He was tired. Back at his office, the hajji's secretary smiled and asked, "What are my orders?"

The hajji looked at him angrily: "You're laughing at the mess I've gotten into, aren't you? You've got the right. I behaved stupidly."

"But why? You're actually helping in the progress of Yemen."

"How so?"

"You're saving a child and can make him an enemy of the existing order now in Yemen. You're rearing a revolutionary who will tomorrow destroy the darkness there."

"*You* will "rear" him."

The secretary smiled, swallowing the insult the hajji had thrown in his face, and said, "No, you will rear him."

"As if I migrated to Ethiopia only to rear bastards. No way!"

"But what will you say to Sayyid Amin?"

The hajji did not answer, but said to himself: *Let his God save the child. I did not create him; it is He Who created him.* He sank into deep thought.

The secretary continued his typing, but inside, he laughed at the hajji. Ever since he had heard of the sayyid's story, he had sarcastically repeated it to everyone he encountered as a way to get back at the hajji for all the times the man had insulted him. Though he had worked for him a long time, the hajji still often made a fool of him in public and many times had threatened to fire him. Still, the secretary knew the hajji could not manage without him, and he also knew that his power over his employer bothered the hajji.

They were very different in their political views. Whenever the hajji began a fundraising campaign, the secretary went all over the Marqatah, making jokes and off-hand comments, but now he felt that the matter was serious. Now it concerned the fate of a child. The secretary smiled. He himself was of mixed blood, so he harbored no ill feelings toward this child whom he had not seen. In fact, he loved the boy, for, like the boy, he had been born without a country, a stranger in a strange land. He used sarcasm as a weapon, a way of justifying his feelings of alienation. The secretary's father dreamed of his homeland, of a future in Yemen, someday when it was "liberated" from oppression. He had a foundation to stand on and dreams to support him. He wasn't a stranger, despite being an expatriate. He had a country to go home to one day. But, his son the secretary was like a rootless tree; he was no one. Yes, no one.

The secretary's mother also had her dreams, her roots. She had a land and a country here in Ethiopia, soil that kindly contained her. But he was the stranger; he could not even say he was a Yemeni, for he did not know Yemen. He had never seen it. He had heard a great deal about it, but did not know it. If he went there, how would it receive him? Would it spit him out as this land had, even though it was his mother's homeland?

Then who was he? They called him muwallad, "half-breed." Where was his land? Who were his people?

So, the secretary felt kindly toward the boy. The only difference was that his Yemeni father acknowledged him, whereas the other boy's father rejected him. He decided he would take him in after all, but as a brother. They were in the same situation and belonged to the same people. They were the lost ones who were stuck in the middle, pulled by both sides. They would always be strangers, even if they finally found a place to grant them refuge.

The hajji looked at the secretary and said, "Have you figured out a solution?"

With a smile on his lips and a heart full of love, the secretary said, "Yes, I've decided to take him as my brother. My younger brother."

The hajji looked surprised: "But…!"

"I've decided, and frankly it is not to save his soul or to make him a Muslim; this is something he has to decide for himself when he is old enough. I don't want him to be a stranger. Do you know what it means to be without roots? Well, I do. So, yes, he'll be my brother. Oh, if only all the half-breeds could find a savior, if only they could decide to find an end to this labyrinth in which they're lost!"

Surprise lingered on the hajji's face. It was the first time he'd heard such serious talk from his secretary. He asked him: "You mean, you half-breeds are without a country?"

"Perhaps that's what I meant; perhaps not. We're a new kind of people. We have special looks and a special existence. We don't know you. You dream of a myth, but we live a reality! You talk twenty-four hours a day about freeing your homeland, but you will never liberate it. You ran away. From here you will never do anything but shout at the top of your lungs, 'You despot, we will revolt.' But you're just opening your mouths, and no one hears you but us. And we're surprised by your pain. We smile when we hear you shouting for liberation, because you've never convinced us of the reality of the freedom for which you fight. Liberating your country requires first that you liberate yourselves, that you not cower, that you fight your enemy face to face."

"Are you crazy?" the hajji objected. "We work here to feed our people back home; we migrated to save our country." In a biting tone, he added, "I know you half-breeds don't care about our concerns. You don't understand that we have to liberate our country first. You came to be a burden on us."

"No, sir, you didn't come to liberate your country. You escaped from the ghost of the Imam. You were afraid. If you really wanted to liberate your country, why did you get married and have children? I tell you frankly, you'll never be the ones to liberate your country. If it is liberated, it will be by those who stayed there, or perhaps by us."

"You?"

"Yes, us! We're searching for a homeland, a nation, a hope. You don't know what it's like to feel like a stranger. We'll try to liberate the land of Yemen. We might succeed, but we will never make the excuse that others are blocking our way."

The hajji laughed. "Do you know that there is a book that says, 'The Ka'aba will be destroyed by people coming from Ethiopia, who have no real ties to Ethiopia except for having been born there?'" They would forget their religion, drink alcohol, and run after women. They would destroy the Ka'aba (the structure in Mecca that symbolizes Islamic ideals).

The secretary smiled. "Yes, we will destroy the Ka'aba, but which Ka'aba? We will destroy the Ka'aba of injustice, corruption, and feudalism. We will destroy the myth you ran away from. We will bring back tranquility. Don't worry; God will protect the real Ka'aba but not the one that enslaves people who were born free. As for us abandoning our religion, drinking alcohol, and chasing women, you know very well that there's no difference between you and me in this matter, only that each of us has his friends and his special meeting places. Our roads are different, but our destination is the same, isn't it?"

The hajji lowered his eyes. He was unaware that his secretary knew about him all these years, but what shook him now was how frank his secretary was being, as though the hajji's latest troubles had stripped away a wall between them.

"What do you want in return for taking in the child?" the hajji asked.

"Just for you to take another look at reality," the secretary replied.

Winter fell on Addis Ababa. Cold winds blew over Sodset Kilo, and the citizens disappeared like black ghosts into their homes each night. Only the drunks remained in the streets, their bellies full of fiery liquor.

Abdou Sa'id shivered inside his store. It was close to nine. He thought of going to the villa, and a tingling feeling ran through his veins. It would be warm there, and there would be a warm body, too. He glimpsed the ghost of a drunk embracing a tree and murmured a prayer. He suddenly decided to close the store.

He shivered as he performed ablutions for his evening prayers. Afterward, he stretched out on his bed and began to dream of his return. Just days before, he'd written a letter to the village, telling them he was coming home, but not giving a specific date. *Let them wait.* He smiled. The villagers would talk about him now and await his return. He envisioned the village before him, just as he'd left it fifteen years ago. He smiled; he knew that they would gawk at anyone who appeared on the road and say, "Here comes Abdou Sa'id."

They would concoct legends about him, that he was a man of worth, real worth. He was shivering, but the kerosene stove warmed his bones. He wanted to go to the villa, but was afraid her husband might be there. He hadn't seen her in days. The last time he went there she said she was tired and that she would send her maid to him if she wanted him to come. Her maid had never shown up.

At that moment his mind turned to Ta'atto. Whenever he thought of her, he felt the heat on his cheeks, but he could not forget her. Though she had gotten him into trouble, he was grateful to her now because she was the reason that Hajji Abdul Latif's secretary had adopted his son, and he had gotten rid of that problem forever. Moreover, he felt inexplicably tied to this woman about whom he hadn't thought since the day he made her a woman. Back then she was just an adventure, one of many women, but she had become something different. He realized that he had missed something, but soon all these thoughts would disappear when he returned to his village.

He knew nothing about life there, and Hajji Abdul Latif and Saleh Saif's talk had made him mistrust the situation for the first time. After giving up on the idea that Abdou would adopt his son, the hajji had said, "You're trying to leave Ethiopia in a hurry, but be sure to pay all the taxes that you owe to the governor and the soldiers in the village. That is, if you don't lose everything."

Lose everything, how? Was that possible? Then what had been the point in emigrating here at all?

The hajji claimed that many emigrants preferred to emigrate again rather than remain at home, that some of them lost everything in courts and conflicts. But he would not go to courts or fight with anyone. He was just a simple human being who wanted to live quietly, worshipping his God and sowing his land. His entire reason for emigrating was so that one day he could go back to his village, work his father's land with his own two hands, and water it with his sweat. Was it possible he might not find that?

No, it couldn't be. They were just jealous of him. Otherwise why did they make all the fuss about the child and his adoption? They simply did not want him to leave. He did not get involved in politics; he had never been against the Imam. Each year he sent his family the taxes that were due the Imam, the country's leader. True, in some of their letters his family complained that taxes were high, but that was not bad. He paid them anyway.

He smiled. No matter what, he would go back to see for himself. He would return to his son and wife and joke about those he'd left behind, those who were jealous of him. Was his wife old now, he wondered? So old he wouldn't recognize her? What was wrong with that? He was rich. He would let his wife rest. If he saw a young woman he liked, he would marry her, and she could wait on him and his wife, who had suffered for him. His good religion allowed him to marry two, three, and four wives; he was a rich man, able to afford it. What a wonderful life he would live. He would go out one day to the fields. He would shepherd sheep and cows. He would have milk and ghee. He would forget the stench of this store. Damn this cold, he thought. What's to be done? He did not want the stove to consume more kerosene.

Abdou Sa'id stood and carried out a tank half-filled with dirt and ashes. He brought in charcoal, closed the door, and doused the charcoal with kerosene so that it ignited quickly and warmed up the place. He stretched out on his bed, but could not sleep.

The red blaze coming from the stove excited him. He remembered that when he was a child, how the village would celebrate the return of someone from abroad with a huge feast. When he returned he would hold the biggest party the village had ever known; he would make them talk about him not for days, but for months on end. He had worked very hard, and it was time to rest. A smile poured over his lips. He felt warm. Sleep flirted with his eyes.

The charcoal began to glow red, sending up spirals of smoke. The blaze died after absorbing all the kerosene, and smoke poured out silently.

Abdou Sa'id dreamed that he had returned to his village. The roads were filled with people. Children raced by with smiles on their faces. He opened a sack he was carrying and handed out sweets to them.

Joyfully, the children shouted, "Abdou Sa'id, Abdou Sa'id!"

He whispered something in the ear of one of the children and poured out a handful of sweets. He rushed into the village. Dozens of half-naked children tramped after him. In the village someone cried, "Which house is the most beautiful?"

They shouted behind him, "That one is! That one!"

He looked ahead, to the heart of the village, as the men came out to receive him. Women stood upon rooftops or at the corners of their homes, looking at him shyly. In their eyes, he saw many things. The men greeted him respectfully, their voices flattering. The old women moved toward him, saying, "May God protect you!" "May God glorify you!" Women strewed flowers in his path.

Abdou Sa'id smiled at them all. He was clad in his silk gown and the woolen jacket he'd had taken in yesterday by the best tailor. On his head he wore an elaborate head cover. He had a staff in his hand, a gown over his shoulders, and a smile on his lips.

He dreamed and smiled while smoke filled the cramped room.

"Who is the richest man in the village?"

The village children shouted, "He is! He is!"

Cracks of gunfire welcomed him, and they slaughtered a sheep by the door of his house. He spotted his wife, modestly hiding near one of the roads. She was shy, but he would see her at night. Men entered the guest hall. Women came in to visit his wife and busied themselves unloading the six donkeys that carried the presents he had brought from Aden. "You will have dinner with us," he told his neighbors. He sent someone to buy qat—no, no, he would bring the qat with him.

Abdou coughed, but the dream was beautiful. Children's shouts mixed with the cracks of gunfire.

Nearby villagers asked, "Whose wedding is it?"

News quickly spread: "Abdou Sa'id is back from overseas."

His smile grew wider. He stirred on his wooden bed. His coughs got louder. It was about one in the morning; heat ran through Abdou Sa'id's store. Smoke billowed out from the charcoal. Abdou dreamed on. He turned, and in his mind heard children's voices:

"What house is the best in the village?"

"Abdou Sa'id's."

"There he is, there he is!"

"Whose land is this?"

"It belongs to Abdou! There he is!"

"Whose gun is the best?"

"Abdou's!"

❧   ❧   ❧

In the morning customers waited for the store to open, but in vain. Some were worried. Others merely smiled. They whispered at first and then began to openly speculate: "What happened?"

"Perhaps he's sick."

"Don't say that. Perhaps he's at his friend's in the Marqatah."

"But that's never happened before."

Some shook their heads; people started to gather outside the store. They shouted, "Abdou, Abdou!"

The store was locked from inside. Something had happened to the man.

The women's eyes grew wide with apprehension.

"One of the Yemenis should come to see what's the matter."

"Or let's call the police. Perhaps there was a robbery?"

Another quietly added, "Or a murder."

Women's voices rose, saying, "God forbid, God forbid."

From inside came the sound of soft painful sighs. A woman pressed her ear close to the door, gesturing to the crowd to be still. "Keep quiet for a moment. I might be able to hear something." Seconds later she said, "I hear moaning; the man is sick. We've got to get some Yemenis here."

"Maybe it's something contagious."

One of them rushed to a nearby store and told the Yemeni owner what had happened.

It was nighttime when they took Abdou Sa'id to the hospital. A man went to the Marqatah to tell Saleh Saif, who in turn rushed to Sodset Kilo after finishing his work. But Abdou Sa'id was unable to talk. He was faint; his eyes bulged; his lips were pressed tightly to each other, as if he didn't want to talk, or as if he had suffered some terrible torture.

When the doctor saw him, he tore open Abdou's clothing and spat out two harsh comments: "Primitive people! How can they live in this filth?"

No one understood what he said except the nurse, who smiled and replied, "But they live."

The doctor added, "To die like animals."

The news spread all over Sodset Kilo. The giant was dead, the one who had stood on his own two feet on his little square plot for more than a dozen years. He'd finally fallen. Many tears were shed. At night, candles were lit in the prostitutes' bedrooms; inside those walls were human hearts gentler than virtue itself.

Ta'atto herself lit two candles and knelt before the picture of St. George holding his spear to pierce the heart of the ugly dragon. If someone had passed by that night, he would have felt the sorrow that had fallen upon the women of the quarter, would have heard the prayers of those women who had only yesterday cursed Abdou Sa'id. That evening in Sodset Kilo, hundreds voiced love for that man, for no other reason than that he was like them, had suffered much silently, and also because he was a stranger, a kind stranger with a constant smile.

Could it be true that sickness had brought him down in just one night? Ta'atto believed it was her anger and the saint Sayyid Amin that had brought him down though she hadn't wanted that to happen. She did not know why, but she loved him. All night the doctor sat by Abdou's bedside. "He fought bravely against a huge amount of carbon dioxide," he said to the nurse. "If he'd been able to hold out until morning, I'd have been able to save him. What agony he must have suffered."

The nurse was acquainted with Abdou and told the doctor what she knew about him. The doctor was an Italian who adored Ethiopian women. When he heard what the nurse said, he exclaimed, "How, by God, could he live in this hell? This is terrible."

"But what else can these people do? These migrants leave their homes, country, family, to chase after a living. They die running after scraps. That's all they think about."

"You say they left their land. Yes, but why? Because they couldn't stand against adversity. A nation that emigrates from its land is a nation of traitors."

"Injustice makes treason easy."

"But it doesn't justify running away."

Unfortunately, Abdou Saʻid could not hear this conversation. If he could, he would have opened his eyes, amazed. What were these crazy people talking about? He would have told them of the fabulous world of his dreams, the one that had become his alone and forever. It was better than anything they could ever hope to create.

The giant fell. When the doctor covered his ice-cold body, he said, "He died because he endured more than he should have. It was a worthless life, and didn't deserve to be lived." But if the doctor had known Abdou's dreams, he might have felt differently.

The funeral was simple, exactly like the life of Abdou Saʻid, but the pain tore at the hearts of two women: one was a lonely woman who sat in her room beneath a photo, burning two candles. The other lay on a bed of silk; inside her grew a baby whose father had died just the day before.

The residents of the Marqatah gathered around the coffin of Abdou Saʻid who lay in his final resting place, his last palace, a simple grave. Here no children shouted, "The most beautiful tomb in the world is Abdou Saʻid's!"

Hajji Abdul Latif stood silently over the grave, covering it with earth. He looked at the tree near the grave. To his secretary he said, "He found a grave I dreamed of."

His secretary looked at him and smiled. "Are graves the final outcome of all this struggle?"

"What do you mean?" asked the hajji, annoyed.

"I mean that graves are a good place to bury certain movements. You know when he died he left nothing behind. A woman deserted for years there, a son he didn't know, a land to which he didn't offer a drop of his blood. He died like a stranger, like hundreds of Yemenis die in other lands. As for this grave—it's not his. It's not his land; it belongs to other people, to the Ethiopians. We even occupy their graveyards. As if it's not enough to swallow the meager scraps meant for their mouths, we occupy their graves, too. Oh God, we are such strangers!"

But no one listened. The hajji approached the grave to recite the introductory Al Fatiha chapter of the Quran. People scattered throughout the graveyard. They talked about many things that had nothing to do with the man over whom they had spread the earth.

The secretary carried Abdou Sa'id's son away and pointed to the graves, saying: "Look, my little one. Here, all over this graveyard, strangers sleep forever. This land did not give birth to them, did not rear them, but it killed them. They cheated their own land, so they forfeited their right to be buried in it. Blessed is the man who's buried in his own soil, in his homeland."

The little boy looked at the secretary, understanding nothing; suddenly tears rolled down the secretary's face, so the little boy joined him in crying.

"As for us, my little one," said the secretary. "Where's our land? We are even more strangers than they are. We have no land. We are the most lost of all."

He and the boy were the last ones left at the cemetery. Before they left, they took one final glance around the place, standing in the shadows cast by fragrant trees.

From one corner of the graveyard, a woman rushed to the grave. Her clothes were black, her eyes full of tears. She carried flowers.

"Look, it's Ta'atto." The child ran to hug her.

The secretary stood still, watching them cry together. Inside him something was about to burst.

Would they finally find their true path in life? Here was a woman in her black dress, putting flowers on the grave of this man. Though it was distorted by sadness, her face was still beautiful. What did she think of this stranger who had died, who left nothing but his grave?

The woman and the child approached and he smiled sadly. He realized something he did not know before.

At sunset, three ghosts left the graveyard.

Stories

The Ghoul

The winds are blowing hard outside, sweet girl. Come nearer. I want to tell you a tale… Listen to me carefully. This is a story that I heard when I was a small boy, and all the boys in my village have heard it by now, for it's the story of our victory. It's about the ghoul in our mountain.

I don't know when the story began, but they say that a ghoul came to our mountain, where he found a terrible, large cave. Today this cave has become a place for lovers. In this cave, sweet girl, I met my first love, and had my first kiss…

Inside this big, terrible cave used to live the ghoul; nobody knew where he came from, nor why or how. Nobody saw him as he captured his victims, but everybody saw their remains, traces of his many crimes, on the road between our village and the mountain. The people of my village wove myths around him. It was said that he couldn't die, that he wasn't affected by bullets, and that he came to our mountain to take revenge on us, because God was angry with us…

What nonsense did they utter? They repeated all sorts of things among themselves, but they are to be excused for they are ignorant. You know that the people of our village are cowards when they are alone, but bold as lions when they are united.

Many things were said that added to their fears. Can you imagine that? They made up the stories and later they believed them. The ghoul soon became the unchallenged king of the mountain. Every morning the ghoul sent from his cave the bones of his victims, miserable animals or humans whose fates drove them to his jaws and could not be saved. On dark nights, the ghoul would attack our village, break into the livestock pens, carry off whatever he wanted, and return to the mountain. Nobody could stand in his way… He was capable of anything, his power fueled by the myths that grew with every victim. The ghoul could not die, so how could they resist?

Why should they bother themselves with something that seemed to be so real? Why should they fight against their own legends?

As days passed, the ghoul's authority grew, as did the numbers of his victims. He became the king both of the mountain and of the village. He was said to own the souls of those who knelt before him.

As the days passed, new myths were spun and old wives tales revolved around the ghoul...and only the ghoul. Even the children used to repeat foolishly what old women said, and their gaze was always on the mountain.

The winds are blowing hard, the storm is on its way. There is no wood to burn. Oh, my sweet girl, come closer, closer. The ghoul made everything terrible, unbearable, unreal. The mountain changed into something mysterious, not to be controlled by humans.

Oh, the winds are cold, they remind me of the fear that invaded the minds of the villagers as they rushed to bolt their doors by sunset.

At that time, when the ghoul controlled everything, there was a woman, an ordinary woman—a mother who lived in the village. Her name was Hind.

Nobody cared about her, for she was very poor and people don't care much about the poor. She had lost everything, all that she owned: money, land, and jewelry. She had lost everything for the sake of her only son. Yes, sweet girl, she had a son, ten years old, whom her husband had left behind when he died at sea. He was one of the country's courageous adventurers that exist everywhere. Our country's sailors, my sweet girl, made a glorious history for us, a forgotten history that no one knows except the sea itself. Oh, how great are those who die quietly after leaving behind tragedies. He died leaving his wife and child alone. The child became sick, and Hind had to sell all that she owned for medicine. She prayed and prayed, visited the tombs of all the saints, but the gates of heaven did not want prayers or visits to saints; they wanted a deed performed. Hind, the poor woman, didn't know that. Slowly she lost everything. Nothing was left but one thing: her body. She wanted to sell it in the slave market, but our village, as any other small village in our country, did not have a slave market. Besides, she had no great beauty… Oh, Lord, she was an ordinary woman, without any beauty—all she had was her heart, her work, her struggle.

She lost hope. She could do nothing but sit next to her child, cleaning his jaundiced face with her tears.

Are the winds still blowing outside, sweet girl? I'm not finished with the story yet.

If there is something remarkable about great people, it is that they act without planning. Hind started to shift between reality and fantasy. As tears streamed down her face, she dreamed that the medicine for her son was there in the cave, in the mountain where the ghoul sleeps, that it was in the black heart of the ghoul, that heart which was filled with the blood of so many others. In that heart lay the medicine.

Hind didn't think. She just found herself in front of the cave's mouth without knowing how she got there. She was moved by that mysterious power, the power of motherhood, which cannot be expressed or described with our simple words. Hind—the broken-hearted, poor, and frail woman—found herself alone at the door of the ghoul whose terror conquered the hearts of all the men in our village.

And in so doing, Hind killed the myth. The ghoul could not believe that a human being would dare to violate his territory and come to his cave. It was a challenge to the creature's power and reputation. Enraged, the ghoul stood to his full height and was astonished to see a short pale woman, so weak and emaciated she was about to collapse. That enraged the ghoul further, to discover that the trespasser was a mere woman, and not some other, stronger being. His pride was sorely wounded.

But Hind was not scared; rather, her power and daring increased when she saw the ghoul's ugly face. She gathered her courage, determined not to leave unless she was carrying the ghoul's heart in her hands, victorious.

The sun shone down strongly, the trees danced, and the small birds sang as they saw this woman challenging fate and breaking down myths that others had created.

"Why are you here, old woman?" the ghoul asked.

"Oh, ghoul, whatever you are and regardless of your power, I am a mother searching for medicine for my son. I know the cure is nothing more or less than your heart, so I came to seize it whether you like it or not."

All of the anger of the world at that moment gathered in the face of the ghoul as he heard the woman's words. Who was she to challenge him? "Oh, you old woman, listen to me. You are the first to ever break my peace and challenge my strength. I vow to destroy you and make you a laughing stock. I will not leave a trace of you on this earth."

But Hind had come this far in breaking through the myth and she felt she must fight on for her son.

If she became frightened or begged for mercy, that would mean her end, so she ignored what the ghoul had just said. She smiled sarcastically, hatred for that grotesque creature which spread fear everywhere glimmered in her eyes.

"You're just a base creature who was created by people who weave a lie you chose to believe. As for me, I'll get your heart whether you let me do it quietly or not!"

The ghoul tried to laugh, but his laughter was dead, cold, and he felt he should do something before he crumbled under her bold gaze.

"Old woman, you don't know how to evaluate your strength; perhaps madness drove you to this adventure. Out of mercy, I'll forgive you this time. Don't forget whose presence you are in, the super-powerful one who is feared by all, the king of the mountain and the village, the victorious, the one who never dies…"

He knew he was lying, and so did Hind.

"Who are you for us to fear? Who are you that we must surrender to you and put our necks under your feet?"

Hind began to walk towards the heart of the ghoul. Terror gathered all at once in the face of the ghoul; yes, terror—*not* courage…

Alarmed, the ghoul fearfully attacked. Hind did not falter, but grabbed him with her hands, her eyes shining.

Oh, if you could only understand the epic courage of the woman as she struggled for the sake of tomorrow, so that others could live happily!

Oh, sweet girl, if you could only have seen Hind when she fought that ghoul, that myth which fell apart, in order to get back to her son and to give him life.

The world was asking: Who will win? The human or the ghoul? Birds stopped singing, the sun became yellowish, as though holding its breath in the sky, trees stopped rustling, the winds were still. Even the mountain, which belonged to the ghoul, held its heart in its hands waiting for its liberation...

Blood ran, sweet girl; the ghoul let out a final shriek and collapsed, defeated. Nature sang the song of salvation, the great song. The mountain poplars danced to the rhythm of the wind, and birds sang. The sun extended its golden hands, saluting Hind's victory.

Hind stood up. Her black dress was torn to shreds, and blood was splattered all over her young body... Her body was the most beautiful in the world at that moment, for it was full of power... Her straight black hair, which she had never taken care of, hung loose over her shoulders, drops of blood dripping from it. She looked around her as she clutched the ghoul's heart in her hands. She began to walk very fast back to the village, to her son. Everything around her was singing and dancing. Next to the mouth of the cave lay the king of yesterday. In a dark corner inside the village, in a humble broken home, the man of tomorrow was stirring.

The storm is over, sweet girl, and my story has ended, too...

Let us embrace one another. We won. Oh, sweet girl, the sun is sending its golden rays on our mountain. The sky is laughing joyfully. Let us smile... Let us smile...

Brother, Are You Going to Fight Them All?

It happened in the morning. I was so tired that morning, I didn't go to work. I was sure my wife and children would go to my father's house, and I was looking forward to being alone, enjoying an ordinary day away from the children's noise and play, and away from work.

As they left, I hurried back to bed. The weather was cold, and my bed was nice and warm.

Moments passed and I began to dream of a quiet, wonderful day of relaxation: perhaps I'd read something, after having quit reading for years. How could I read with four children around? Just one of them equaled a whole marketplace of commotion. And, I always came home from work very tired.

I heard knocking on the door. It started gently but soon grew stronger.

Perhaps, one of the neighbors was looking for something. But the knocking was followed by a voice that was harsh and demanding; I trembled. I climbed out of bed and cursed my attempt at rest, which seemed doomed from the very start. I began to wish my wife and children hadn't left.

I opened the door. A man stood there, his gun slung over his shoulder. His sarong was as short as a mini-skirt, and on his head was a turban as high as the sky. I noticed that he was barefooted.

"Come to the police station."

I was surprised by his harsh tone. "What's the matter?" I asked.

Without even looking at me, he barked: "I said, come with me to the police station."

"But why? What for?"

He shouted back, "Come now!"

I felt my blood start to boil inside me. I slammed the door in his face and said, "For God's sake, go away and don't shout at me. I have no problems with anyone."

But, he began knocking again, and, this time, the knocking was even more intense. The voice was getting louder, shouting even. "This man is cursing the government...humiliating the government representative; everyone bear witness. He slammed the door in the face of government!"

So I went out with him. Children had gathered, and then women, followed by some men, who all looked at us curiously. The soldier didn't give me a chance to talk, but grabbed me by the collar. I lost my composure. "Oh, Muslims, bear witness, this man is attacking me in my home. My God, there is no more sanctity in this country!"

He shouted, "Who told you to humiliate the government? Who do you think you are?"

People tried to intervene. Words flew back and forth. Everyone was trying to find a solution, without even knowing what was going on...

After some moments of total confusion, the soldier himself was beginning to become a victim; people were begging him to be nice to me—and begging me to cooperate.

I heard voices yelling excitedly.

"Go with him to the police station."

"Why don't you want to go? Do you have something to fear?"

"He's the government representative and so you should go with him."

I shouted back, "Listen, everyone! I'm the one victimized here! There's no dispute between me and anybody else. So why did this soldier knock on my door this morning? I don't know what's going on."

One friend shouted at me, "Why did you slam your door on him? Who are you? Who do you think you are to resist a government representative? Or do you think there is no government? I swear, if these people weren't around, you'd see what I'd do to you."

People intervened again...

"Oh, Faarea, come on," they said to me. Let's go together to the police station and see what's the matter..."

I found myself in my pajamas going with the soldier, who walked in front of me, his head raised victoriously. A group of adults and children followed, whistling and laughing.

We arrived at the police station, and I found myself surrounded by a group of friends who had heard what happened. I became a toy in their hands; each took me from one office to the other, until we made it to the proper official. I was miserable.

"What's the matter," the official asked.

"This man refused your summons, sir," answered the soldier. "And he cursed and called the government bad names and humiliated me in front of these people." He pointed to the crowd that had come with us.

Without asking anybody what was going on, the police chief shouted at me. "Who do you think you are? Put the handcuffs on his hands and imprison him." The soldier started to push me again.

But, my neighbors intervened. They begged the officer to wait. They said, "He's a good man, a father of many children; he was tired; he didn't mean anything…"

The police officer was finally convinced and asked to have me returned to him. The cuffs were still on my hands, and my clothes were torn.

"What's your name?"

"Faarea Ali Saed."

"Why did you refuse to come?"

"I swear, I didn't. All I said was that there was nothing between me and anybody else, no disputes or problems, and that I was surprised that he was asking me to go to the police station for no reason."

He turned to the soldier. "What do you want from him?"

"Sir, it was you who ordered me to bring him in."

The officer was surprised. "I…but how?"

He thought for a moment, then finally said, "Oh…"

He searched around for something, a notebook maybe, and said, "I asked you to bring Faarea Saed Ali, the butcher, whom the people complained about, for selling beef and claiming it's veal…" He turned to me and asked, "Are you a butcher?"

I shouted loudly, "I swear to God, I've never been a butcher in my life. I have a grocery store in the market, everyone knows that."

The officer turned to the soldier. "How did this happen?"

The soldier simply said, "Sir, I asked about Faarea Saed; they pointed to his house."

"But I told you he's a butcher…"

"I swear, I don't know, I asked and they said there he was," he said, pointing at me again.

Some of the people whistled; I was about to faint from fatigue.

Finally, the official said, pointing to me, "Undo his cuffs and let him go."

But the soldier asked, "Sir, what about my dues for bringing him in?"

The officer turned to me and said, "Give him the money and the cost of undoing the cuffs, and then go and may God look after you!"

I tried to say something, but one of my neighbors pushed me, and another whispered in my ear, "Brother, are you going to fight them all, or are you going to let God look after you?"

Ya Khabiir

I was on my way back from Hayfan after spending two days on a law case at the governor's office. As usual, I didn't get any results. The legal procedures would continue, but nothing would be resolved.

It was late in the day. I was walking alone, many worries gnawing at me. I had already chewed more than two bundles of sharari qat, which tossed and turned in my stomach. Although I usually don't like walking alone at night, especially for long distances, I had quelled my fear this time and hit the road with my stick while continuing to chew qat. I felt zeal and hate building up inside me. The cool evening breeze, water flowing into small ponds by the side of the mountain, and the vision of the valley in the distance were combining to create sad and revolutionary tunes in my mind.

"*Ya Khabiir! Ya Khabiir!*" [an address of respect for a learned professional]

I turned and cursed the voice that broke my solitary thoughts. Then I trembled slightly when I saw a man. He ran after me barefooted, wearing a short sarong and carrying a gun. His eyes were red from chewing qat.

"Where are you going, ya khabiir?" [An address of respect for a learned professional.]

"To Qutabah," I answered, a sense of loathing filling me. As much as I hated death, I detested soldiers even more.

"Then we're on our way together!"

I continued on my way, followed by the soldier. All the thoughts in my head vanished; only the sound of the soldier's footsteps remained as they forcefully hit the earth. I turned back from time to time to look at him. Adrenaline began to rush through my blood. I hate soldiers. I fear them and have never walked with any of them. Common stories that spread throughout our village about their savage and brutal violence now led me to believe that this man intended to kill me. What would prevent him from doing so? He might think that I had a lot of money. What would stop him from doing away with me? There was no one here to see us. The road was deserted. We had reached the middle of the mountain, and the nearest houses were far away at the bottom of the valley or at the top of the mountain. He had a gun while I had nothing but a thin stick.

The idea began to grow in my thoughts so much that I imagined seeing the soldier take his gun off his shoulder; I imagined the sound of his footsteps to be the sound his gun made as he cocked it to shoot. I stopped by the side of the road, pretending to pull out a thorn in my foot so that he would go ahead of me, but he stopped after a step or two and looked at me. I wished he would just go on, but he waited.

"Do you have a thorn?"

Then, as he looked up at the evening sky, he said thoughtfully, "It's a bit dark. You won't be able to see."

I nodded my head in agreement.

He walked ahead of me this time and I could hear him breathe, letting out a pained sigh from time to time. He tried to hum a sad Sanaa tune, but soon he stopped and, instead, resumed sighing.

He was tall and broad-shouldered, with a tribal manliness about him. He looked as though he could carry the mountain on those shoulders. He swung the gun as if it were a feather. The thud of his feet on the ground was so strong that I imagined the earth to cry painfully.

"Why don't you talk?"

"What do you want me to say?"

I was still afraid of him. I saw his head move as he put more qat in his mouth. From behind the clouds, the light of the moon crept softly. I heard the man's voice; it was simple and deep, with some harshness of the northern accent.

"Ya Khabiir, did you have a law case? My God, what's it with you people from Hujariyyah, that makes you love going to court? Any one of you who has two coins in his pocket files a lawsuit. Why can't you live in peace like the rest of God's creatures without such headaches?"

As he was talking, he scratched his head as if he were contemplating a very difficult problem, then continued. "Or do you think that there's justice only through the regional governor, and not through the local officials? Justice is dead; it was eaten by those with fat bellies. As for you, you civilians, you take a hundred or two hundred riyals and pour them right into the mouths of these fat bellies like bottomless pits. While *our* stomachs are empty, right?"

I couldn't answer him, for the last thing I expected him to talk about was justice, courts, and fat bellies. We civilians had come to see the soldiers as a force for repression and injustice. They were the ones who carried out the governor's orders. We Yemenis could never forget how the soldiers abused us.

But the soldier didn't wait for my answer. He sucked on the qat in his mouth and said, "You live here in Qutabah and I live in Hashid. There I have a home, a family, a wife and children, thank God. But we have no money, no land. The sheiks took our land from us, and we became soldiers trying to get an income. They said there was gold in Hujariyyah. We came here. But, I swear to God, there is nothing here but greed, looting, and envy. Everybody here wants to rob his brother, his friend. Yes, you may have money, but you have no honesty, no morals, no love or care. I swear if I died back home it would be much better. At least then I would be near my wife and children. True, we would still be looking for work and be hungry. But we wouldn't be filing lawsuits against each other. Those fat bellies only got fat with your money."

As I neared him I asked, "Okay, but why do you loot and steal from people?"

He sighed deeply and said, "Loot and rob people? Not all soldiers loot and steal, Ya Khabiir. But, I say that whoever does loot and steal is no worse than the governor. You give the governor one hundred riyals under the table, but if you give a soldier one riyal, you say the soldiers looted and robbed you. Look, the soldier is no different from you; another governor steals from him in his own hometown, both justly and unjustly."

He stopped and looked at the sky; then he unloaded his gun from his shoulder and turned to me. He said, "It's evening, time for the evening prayer. Will you be the imam and lead the prayer?"

"No, you lead the prayer."

He smiled at me, as if we were close friends and said, "Now don't say later that a soldier led the prayers at gun point, okay?"

We laughed.

After the prayers, we continued on our way. All the while, he talked about everything, his wife whom he hadn't seen for three years, his children...

"Sir, I swear to God, I wish that my children would be educated and not become ignorant soldiers like me. But where are the schools? We only have a local fellow, a local teacher, a religious *faqeeh*. These people are even worse than governors. All they care about is money. As God is my witness, I tell you, they don't know the meaning of the Quran. They lie to us. They corrupt this world with their lies."

As we walked, the evening breeze blew gently on us, moving the plants to and fro. My friend talked about Hashid and Sanaa.

I saw my village in the distance, and before I knew what I was saying, I said, "Ya Khabiir, you have a long way to go to reach Mafliss, and this is a moonless night; you should stay with us and leave in the morning."

He studied me for some time and with a gentle smile on his lips said, "Hey civilian! I'm a soldier and we have needs—chicken, qat, a water pipe..."

"And a fee, too?" I quickly added.

He laughed at that.

As we entered the house my family looked at me fearfully. For if a soldier was with me, that meant a crisis and misery must be imminent.

The Chinese Road

Hundreds of bodies were bent forward, facing the ground, each carrying a load of heavy stones and rocks. The sun beating down on the carefully balanced loads made all the heads ache. The workers threw their loads down out of the way and rushed back quickly for more. The tall mountain lay proudly and quietly before the workers carving out the new road. Hands rose to wipe sweaty brows. The workers looked toward the foot of the mountain where some men had gathered to measure. They raised their heads toward the peak of the mountain and smiled. Then they turned back again to pickaxes that beat the earth and drills that whined as they cut violently into the rough rock.

Ali Tuhami raised his head for the hundredth time and looked at the mountain. He nodded as if something were bothering him, something that he couldn't digest. His fellow Yemenis were similarly perplexed. One of the foreign workers, short men with small eyes, which Tuhami imagined had been slit with a knife, passed in front of him. The man's glittering, black hair covered his forehead.

Ali Tuhami smiled as he saw the man running, thick ropes in his hands. The man looked like a sweet, lovable child. Actually, Ali considered that these short men were children, Certainly no more than ten years old. But the deeds they accomplished were greater than even Ali, a tribal man who had lived his forty years among Tuhama's sand, could believe. Ali lived behind the mountain with his tribal chief; they might battle for an *imam's* support or steal from a caravan, or they sailed on the Red Sea in small boats carrying anything and stopping in front of any seaport…

Ali was an adventurer. But those small children, who had come from China to help his countrymen build the first road across the mountains to the capital city Sanaa, which he had never seen, were more than adventurers. Those children, as far as he was concerned, were crazy.

He raised his head toward the sun. It sent back harsh burning rays, but his tall black body had gotten used to these rays. The mountain directly in front of him looked like a stumbling block in the road leading to Sanaa.

The mountain was rough rock, hard without any tracks of life. Ali watched as ropes were tied around the waists of the short men who, without delay, began to climb the mountain. His heart started to beat strongly and then everything became apparent. He had not been able to believe the news some days ago, when he heard that the Chinese were blowing up all of the mountains that hindered the road's straight path. But how could these madmen blow up a mountain, he had wondered.

The men climbed quickly, and many heads were raised upward toward them. Bodies stood erect and faces showed surprise as the people of the town saw for the first time in their lives men climbing the rocks like monkeys. Not only that, they were working as they went. The workers carried strange-looking shovels to make holes at the heart of the mountain. The short men's hands trembled from fatigue, but they did not stop walking. What strange, childlike men!

Ali remembered his days when he was a slave of "Hadi Haig." He worked with another group of strange people then. Their faces were always red and they sweated profusely and drank non-stop. He would watch them, while they watched him and all his coworkers as they planted their master's land together. Those men had tried to avoid Ali and the other servants as much as they could. They slept far away from the villages, in big white tents and sometimes in cars with armed guards around them. They carried long sticks and squinted when they looked at the desert, the sands, the huge mountains, and the green land that was green because of the work and the sweat of Ali and his people. These strangers did nothing but write on big white notepads. After a long time, they went away, leaving nothing behind but the hatred of his people.

Ali got closer to the mountain and watched the Chinese. They broke his heart over and over again. There was a big difference between them and the other strangers; Ali could see that. These were more serious in their work than those with red faces. Both groups were strangers to him. But these with whom he was working today were "work horses," as others would often call them. They were not arrogant, nor did they try to avoid Ali and his colleagues; they all slept in the same camp with them and worked together. And they smiled and greeted everyone, even though it was in broken Arabic. They tried to help the farmers and cheerfully admired their labor. Ali remembered the accident on the road, when a boulder had fallen on one of the Yemeni laborers. A Chinese man had rushed quickly to help and had torn his shirt to tie up the man's wound; another came rushing with a medicine box. They had been very kind and helpful to the wounded man.

The Yemenis whispered together as they watched the men, hanging by ropes, moving over the rocks in all directions, working tirelessly. Some felt pity, others fearfully waited for the moment when one might fall. But the Chinese worked efficiently and silently. Ali could imagine the smiles on their faces and he smiled, too.

When work hours were over, the laborers returned to their camps. They were a strange mix—peasants, sailors, shepherds. This was the first time they had done such work—cutting through the mountain to pave a road between Hodaida and Sanaa.

The area where Ali Tuhami was working was one of the largest. Each team of workers had been assigned to a different region. The competition was stiff for which team would finish first. Tuhami's group was in the lead. Suddenly, he heard a noise and saw the laborers quickly disappear. Voices shouted, "A blast…a blast." Two Chinese men stood close to him, looking toward the mountain. Ali saw that the mountain had holes in its side…he got closer to the Chinese men. From far away came the sound of a huge explosion and the earth shook under his feet. Smoke and dust spread, and the mountain shook as it vomited all that was inside it. Moments passed.

Ali Tuhami could not believe what was happening. He could barely hear, and dust surrounded him. Smoke was filling his wide nostrils, his eyes were weeping, but through the tears he saw a big smile, on a small angelic face that had tiny black eyes and a fine nose.

When he fully opened his eyes, the mountain was no longer there…it had become a wide avenue filled with rocks, sand, and smoke. A small voice by his side said, "How is it?…Is it okay?"

He looked at the smiling face next to him. The man was pointing to the mountain that had vanished a moment ago. "The road is complete," he announced.

Tuhami nodded. At that moment all he wished was that his friends who farmed Hadi Haig's land were here to see what he had seen.

The Chinese man and Tuhami stood side by side, looking at the road in front of them. In the distance, the high peaks of other mountains appeared. He asked the Chinese man, "You, how old are you?"

The man's smile widened. He opened his hands three times. Ali couldn't believe it. Everything about the man made him seem no more than 20—his hair, his eyes, and especially his beardless chin.

Then the Chinese man asked, "You, how old are you?"

Ali opened his fists four times.

He walked Ali over to the explosion site. Ali was trying to understand some of what he was seeing. He stopped, pointing to the far-away mountain. The Chinese man understood, and raising his hands in the air, shouted: "All that…finish one day."

The two became friends. Still, several times, Ali mistakenly greeted some other Chinese; they all looked alike and all were smiling.

The teams continued to work quickly and efficiently, without stopping. Chinese experts worked beside them, carrying the shovels, digging and smiling. Their enthusiasm infected everybody. Ali Tuhami, who had once been Hadi Haig's servant, knew he could only admire and respect these strangers. He thought: "If they work this hard in our country, then imagine how they must work in their own country!"

The far-away mountain came closer; it, too, would have to be moved to make way for the road to Sanaa.

Ali's friend smiled as he climbed the new mountain. He shouted to Ali who was handing tools to him, "You and I are stronger than the mountain."

Ali was in awe. For the first time in his life, he realized that a man—actually he himself—could be stronger than the mountain. By the third, and then the fourth mountain, Ali Tuhami was up in front by his friend's side. The mountain rose once more to give way with a blast, opening the road, "China Road," as local people called it. Ali was in the front, the first Yemeni worker to help move the mountain and pave the road. Other Yemenis followed on other mountains, doing the same work as the Chinese, as Ali Tuhami. His Chinese friend smiled, saying, "Yemenis…all smart!"

Nothing New

Dedicated to: M.A.Gh. "My companion on the long road."

Laila didn't know the meaning of the word rest. Every part of her body ached. Work was draining her youth and draining the child that Modhesh had left inside her when he went away. Now, the young, emaciated child was crawling over the room's dirt floor, where a glimmer of light splashed in only by accident. The ancient house was built in the old Yemeni style. The windows were not big enough for a person to see through, but were good for shooting a gun out of. The house was as old as time. One story had collapsed a while back, but Laila made do with what remained. The only music she heard each day was the cow and the sheep in the barn and her own sighs. She managed with one room, just a corner really, using a mat covered by reeds and a torn blanket, its color lost under dust.

It was afternoon, and she went out to water the vegetables. It had rained very little that year. As soon as the plants began to turn green, they withered on the arid land. But, Laila continued to water them daily. Only a bit of grain remained in her store, barely enough to stave off the ghost of hunger. Still, hunger was her reality.

Laila heard her neighbor's voice as she passed in front of the house. She left her son chewing dirt as she spoke to her friend, who was stylishly attired in an almost new dress. From her headdress, which she wore only on special occasions, Laila knew that her neighbor was on her way to visit someone.

"Where are you off to, my cousin?"

The neighbor, as if trying to hide her joy, replied, "They say that the camel caravan leader has arrived from Aden."

Laila's heart suddenly began to beat faster. Perhaps a letter had arrived! Her neighbor offered, "Do you want me to ask if there's a letter for you?"

A long time had passed since Laila had heard from Modhesh; silence enveloped him wherever he was. The mail would not change how heartsick she was, but maybe the caravan leader, with a word or some news could ease her mind?

She nodded in agreement. The neighbor didn't wait; she hurried off to the caravan leader's house. Laila said to herself, *She has the right to be happy, her husband lives in Aden.* Unlike her own husband, who had gone overseas to a faraway land.

Laila couldn't move. Her cow stood near the house. And, the shepherd had brought back her sheep. (She paid annually one quarter of the sheeps' value to the imam as *zaka,* or alms.

Her mind was on the caravan leader's house, with the happy, joyous women, as each of them at this moment were receiving their letters, money, gifts, and clothes.

She looked toward his home, longing to find out about the unknown. In her heart she felt almost certain that this time she would receive some news.

She went to her room where her son was still eating the dirt, his mouth and cheeks smeared with mud. She opened her old trunk and blew off the layers of dust that had accumulated on it. She wanted to take out the dress she wore during the feast, and a headdress that she had folded carefully. She had not worn these clothes for a long time, since the last feast. Modhesh had left during Ramadan two years ago. Her son, who was now crawling next to her, trying to see what was hidden in the wooden trunk, had been born three months after her husband left. Laila wrote that the boy was beautiful and looked just like him. Months later, Modhesh sent her clothes from a place called Ju'afan. He used to send money and clothes whenever he passed through ports. Then, suddenly, nothing. The returning migrants told her he was in a faraway country called America working in coal mines, and that when he returned, he would be carrying lots of money and clothes.

But Laila wanted *him.* She wrote and wrote, though she suspected many of her letters were lost on the way. A war was on, and many ships on which Yemenis worked sunk daily. Her fear grew.

The nights grew longer. She began to have many disturbing nightmares; perhaps he had sunk in a boat, perhaps he was sick, had gotten married, perhaps...

She closed the door. Her neighbor had not returned. The baby's mouth was open; his deep-sunken eyes and his jaundiced face peered at her. Sweet words came from his mouth: "Ma...Ma...Ma."

Though the child was almost two years old, he still could not walk, and his speech was not clear because of malnutrition. He was like his father, she told herself, the silent type.

She heard someone calling out her name—and in that voice there was joy. She rushed to meet her neighbor who was carrying something. Laila's heart beat faster, and her throat became dry. Her mind produced thoughts faster than she could make sense of them.

"The caravan leader had a letter..."

She could not hear the rest. She quickly put on her dress and headdress, grabbed her child and ran out the door, leaving the cow near the house.

Her heart thumped so loudly she thought the other women could probably hear it. Her shyness prevented her from talking.

The caravan leader looked at her, the shadow of a smile on his wizened old face. As he took the letter from his sack, she recognized it by its sweat-stained color.

"Your husband is in good health and he salutes you and his son. He sent you money for house expenses, the livestock, and taxes. He works very hard in America."

He counted out her Maria Teresa riyals. Timidly, she asked, "Didn't he say when he'll be back?"

The old man shook his head and said, "No, he didn't say."

A vein in her heart seemed to rupture, and years she had not really lived grew on her face. Her child looked surprised, as his ears heard the beating of her heart and his hands felt the heat coming from he distraught body. Laila saw a pile of riyals in front of her.

"This is one hundred riyals."

Oh, what would she do with the money? One hundred riyals was a huge amount, but still it was just enough for household expenses for several months. Famine might show up as it did last year and swallow the money and the grains, as well as their souls.

The tax department of the imam had a share in this hundred, perhaps a larger share than her own. The sheik and the headman of the village also had a share.

The caravan leader went to another room. Perhaps he would be back with new dresses.

She turned to see more women than she could count staring at her. The women's faces were dusty and fearfully sad; they were waiting like her for a word, news, dresses… But their husbands had not sent a thing.

The money wasn't going to be enough for her. The state wanted everything. And the rain didn't bring a thing.

One old woman shook her head, "I guess my son's run into more problems than the others. May God save him and provide for him. Usually he was all right, he sent something, at least once a year. But the others are lost; they no longer send even letters. God knows where they are buried."

Laila wasn't listening. She had many problems on her mind. But she would buy meat and chicken tomorrow, so she and her little boy could have a good meal.

For more than three months she hadn't seen the color of meat nor tasted it.

The caravan leader came back carrying in his hands the rest of the things her husband had sent.

"This is a care package from Modhesh: sugar, rice, headdress, dress and clothes and soap. How lucky you are with such expensive gifts."

She hadn't known soap for a year, not tasted rice, for the war had made things scarce.

The child couldn't believe that his mother had brought all these things home. But, her joy wasn't complete, for what she really wanted was his return. She stayed up all night praying for him to have good health and to return safely.

Laila kissed the letter that had come from Modhesh. She told her son that one day he would be able to read the letter himself when he went to Quran school.

Years passed, followed by more years; the letter became tattered from so many kisses and tears…

The Land, Salma

When the clouds began to gather in the sky, Salma ran to open the irrigation canals to water the fields near the house. By the time she came back, the sky had already opened its gates, and rain poured down, feeding the thirsty earth.

Everyone in the house was asleep, and Salma found herself alone in her room. She stretched out on the bed, turning her face toward the open window overlooking the fields. Rainwater was gushing from the canals onto the parched land. But Salma's imagination led her away from the land and the rain toward other things.

She heard a voice whisper: "Salma, finally, you're facing yourself. You must admit the truth; don't try to run away from yourself, for that won't help you. Admit it, you've been waiting for him a long time and you can't bear it any longer. Try to remember how long your husband Dirham has been away. Five years, exactly. Oh, Salma, five years and you're starting the sixth year of waiting. How old are you? Count, you don't need to rush. You're twenty-six years old. Yes, you've started to feel that you're getting old—quickly, without noticing and without enjoying life. Do I have to remind you, Salma, that you were married ten years ago? Yes, your husband went away after leaving a seed inside your womb. He didn't even know. You didn't tell him, as that was the custom of the village. You thought he wouldn't be gone for long."

But he had been gone longer than all the previous times.

"Slow down, Salma. Let's not race ahead of events. Let's begin at the beginning, when you were born. I mean, from when you were married. Am I right?

"Yes, it's clear from your face. You were young then, only sixteen years old, living in your father's house. One day you heard whispering and saw everyone looking at you. You sensed what was going on around you and were happy as every young girl should be happy at the prospect of her wedding. You kept your joy hidden from people so they wouldn't talk about you behind your back.

"But you showed me, I know everything. You were happy to get married to Dirham. When your aunt came, covered your face with a veil, and announced, 'Now your marriage to Dirham is confirmed,' you put up a struggle and called everybody around you names; but deep inside, you were happy. Tears rolled down your cheeks—tears of joy. People thought you were weeping out of sadness for leaving your father and his house.

"When your husband's family arrived to take you to your new home, you walked quickly to get there as soon as possible. People noticed that and you were embarrassed for fear others would discover how eager you were to get to your new home.

"But Salma, did you really love Dirham? No, I don't think you did. Then what was the secret of that happiness of yours? Was it because you were a young girl or that you thought you would be freed from your father's house? From the hard work you did there? Did you think you would find peace and comfort at your husband's house?

"Let's look, Salma, at your new life under your husband's roof. After the first seven days—the wedding days—you began your duty as a wife, to serve her husband and his family.

"You woke up every day before the dawn prayer, milked and fed the cow, then went to the well. After filling your water jar, you came home to fix your husband's breakfast. At noon, you went to the fields to work with your father-in-law, plowing, sowing and clearing, only to return home exhausted to fix lunch: you ground the grain, kneaded the dough, and baked the bread to feed your husband.

"After lunch he left to chew qat. You rarely had lunch, which was usually your breakfast, too: bits of bread with bits of coffee beans or a pudding with milk.

"Then it was after-the-lunch work: washing clothes, going to the mountain to collect firewood, going to the well again at sunset to get the evening water and then cutting grass for the cow. You fixed dinner and offered it to your husband who came home after praying at the mosque. How many times did you forget to pray? You lay down near midnight dead tired and woke up at the dawn prayer call to work again—till you were exhausted.

"This has been your life, every day. Has there been anything new in the last ten years?

"It's the same life you used to live at your father's house. Nothing has changed except your boss—first your father, then your husband. You and Dirham did live together for a while before he left to work in the city. Remember, you encouraged him to leave because you wanted new silk dresses and other presents that husbands usually brought back to their wives after being away.

"Your husband didn't disappoint you; he came back after two years and brought everything you dreamed of. But, your life didn't change whether he was at home or away. In both cases you worked for his family and for the land. Salma, your husband went back to the city, for two years, and then came back again to leave your first baby in your womb. You waited for his return to you and to his child. A year passed. And another. And five years, but still he hasn't appeared. He's still alive overseas, over there. Across the big sea, the one they say has no end.

"How do you know, Salma, whether he's alone or not? Don't tremble and turn pale. It's merely a thought, a guess. He might be alone, and he might not. No one trusts men, especially when they're far away, unseen by familiar eyes. Why should your husband be any different? You know the story of your uncle, Zaid, who deserted his wife for twenty years. He's alive and has another wife and children. They say one day he will return to his first wife, who still waits for him.

"Why won't your husband do the same? Yes, why wouldn't he cheat on you? He's a human being and a man. Men are always weak, as they claim. I say this not to upset you and not to bother you with doubts, but merely as a possibility. The truth is unknown; it's there overseas with your husband.

"Don't think about acting like him, cheating on him. You couldn't, because here in the village people hear every whisper. Haven't you noticed that for the past two days everyone has been following you with their eyes filled with doubt? Haven't you noticed? Why are they throwing those silent looks your way? You're smart, Salma. You know. You're wearing make-up. Yes, make-up. They haven't seen you wear make-up since your husband left five years ago. Don't try to argue that you feel you're getting old and are trying to look young. That's unlikely.

"The truth, Salma, is that you're wearing make-up for him, for Hassan. No, no—don't let your heart flutter. Don't get embarrassed and blush——you'll reveal your secret. See how much you love him?

"There is nothing wrong with loving someone, but it is shameful to betray another. You betray your husband when you love someone else. Yes, it's a very dangerous matter. A woman in your position here doesn't have the right to love whom she wants, nor to enjoy her youth. She is merely a servant. The man marries her to serve his parents. He leaves her to go far away and not come back. She doesn't have the right to seek divorce. Divorce is disdained. Don't put your hand over your breast as though you don't like the thought. Divorce is something you'd like since you would enjoy the life that your husband has stolen. But you couldn't get a divorce. Especially since your father's death there would be no one to support you. Now, you're only a servant of your husband's family, of your husband's father, of your husband's son, and of his land.

"You won't gain a thing by loving Hassan. He's a nice young man, every young woman wants him, but you aren't a young girl. You're a woman with a husband and a child. Are you thinking of those childhood days when you used to play with him in the mountains, and he would take you as his mate when you played the game of husband and wife? Those days are gone. You're old today—five years of waiting have been tough. But, Salma, what can you do?

"Do you ask for divorce? If you do that, where will your child go? And who will marry you?

"You well know that many women live without husbands after they divorce. The young men of the village seek out only the young girls.

"Think about your land, Salma. Yes, it's your land, this land that you give your life for, your youth, your blood. Your land where you've poured your sweat for years. How could you leave your land and for whom?

"You're thinking, Salma. This is good. Nobody values the land like you do. Your husband won't care for the land and neither will your son when he grows up. He'll leave it like his father did. He'll go away like others have.

"Your land, Salma, you've worked for it, shed blood for it. From this land you eat all year long; your son eats and grows because of the land. Even your husband, when he returns, will eat from it. And you…it's you who keeps producing the good things from this land, the grain, the fodder, the milk and the ghee. Everything in this village comes from the land. Isn't the land your life? The life your son will know when he is older and understands the effort you've put into it?

"As for Hassan, he's exactly like your husband. He won't live in the village forever. He'll depart tomorrow, leaving behind a woman to serve his parents, to work the land. Even if you were that woman—what's the difference between your present life and life in his house? There is no difference, Salma, no difference."

❧ ❧ ❧

The voice faded. Salma looked around her, surprised. The rain was falling softly on the land, like the music in dreams. The streams on the mountain's terraces embraced the dry, yellow roots, giving them life.

Her small son opened the door to her bedroom, came in, and threw himself into her arms. Salma fiercely thought, *I'll teach him. I'll teach him to love the land.*

The rainwater seeped slowly into the earth.

The Color of Rain

Are you afraid?"

"No, I'm shivering…maybe it's from the cold…or…" He was silent for a moment and started to stare at the horizon before him. His gaze returned after taking in the black mountain peaks, those mountains that surrounded the deep valley asleep in its mythical silence. It was like his father's brooding silence, before the revolution in Yemen had brought him to this distant peak that echoed with distant gunfire.

"Are you hungry?" the other man said.

"Maybe. I haven't eaten a real meal for days."

"What about some bread?"

"I'm tired of bread."

"You fool! Don't you know how good it tastes? I'm fed up with what you call a real meal. In twenty years I have eaten everything, from snakes in China to frog soup in France…"

"Are you going to tell me all that all over again?" the young man asked.

"But why not?" That way the night will pass more quickly and we won't be bored or afraid."

"Or hungry?"

"Perhaps."

Shots from afar were heard and echoed in the valley; the young man trembled.

"Did I tell you that you're afraid?"

"Please, I just feel cold."

"Look, don't you feel that there's something new going on this evening?"

"What is it?" he asked scared.

"It rained this morning."

"So?"

"Don't you feel that the rain's color cleaned everything, even the moon?" the older man said, pointing to the moon.

"Hey! Trust me, it's better if you leave your hand on the trigger…"

"Oh! Don't you see how wonderful everything is? Have you ever imagined seeing such a beautiful scene?…The moon is sending its light like the rain shower that fell this morning. Even the stars, they look like the beginning of raindrops from clouds. Rain has a color; you can't feel it, but you can see it when you want to see those creatures that fall into it. When I was a sailor, I never thought about the moon or the rain. They would have only made me long for the village. You don't know the meaning of the sea, to spend years on it, the sun barbecues you, and the night swallows you into its silence. I was ready to give my life for a scene like this. Don't you see the mountain peaks in front of us? They're very vivid in all their details. Look over there; I would trade my life for such beauty. Oh, God, I thought that joining the army was just an adventure, that I'd carry weapons and sing songs of the revolution, like the ones I used to hear in French ports about the revolution, Napoleon, 'the Marseillaise.' But did the French ever see anything wonderful like this? The moon reveals everything for you, yes, everything…"

Then he fired his gun, the mountain echoed, and the body by his side trembled.

"What's wrong with you? Are you crazy?" he asked.

"No, no. It's just that the moon's so wonderful. It's lower on the horizon; can't you see that? So I worship the moon, the soft light. It doesn't give you the full picture, the shadows are enough. Don't tremble, my friend. You're just not used to the cold, being from Aden. There the sun is shining all the time, but sometimes it is a bother. You've never seen an iceberg. I've seen, in my twenty years as a sailor, all the seas and heard all the stories. But, that I would be a soldier in the revolution, that is the last story I imagined would happen, but it did."

The young man said, "Listen, friend, I've heard you say this for the twentieth time. But for the first time, you've proved to be a good sniper. You hit something down there. It might be suffering in pain, or maybe it died, I can't tell. I didn't see it move after it fell down." He was silent for a moment and then went on, "But you're repeating all of that again. The moon is the moon, the same one that we see every night with the stars and the rains. There is nothing there except the fact that I sank in mud trying to catch that damn rabbit that showed up this afternoon. I was imagining a delicious meal of grilled rabbit, but got nothing except stale bread!"

↩ ↩ ↩

A cold wind blew, howling as it passed the gap. The mountain echoed the shout of a man. Nobody answered it, the echo died, and the man fell to the bottom and crashed against the rocks in the deep valley.

"Listen, listen, do you feel something?" the young man asked.

It was a scary sound; he pulled the gun near him.

"Don't be afraid, it's the sound of roaring water, it's the flood coming from the north. The clouds covered that whole area this morning. Here come those waters, violently, after all that rainfall, don't you feel its great presence? It's like the roar of soldiers creeping towards the target, fearlessly. They tear silence and cowardliness to shreds. They forget everything, even their existence. They plunge forward, everyone encouraged by the others at his side. If a soldier were alone he might have run away, but they are a crowd, you know, they're more than one person. Don't you hear them crashing against the mountains? Even the falling trees don't bother them. They're compelled. Everyone is encouraging the other, fearlessly, defiantly."

The flood reached the valley. They were lying at the mountain's peak. Water rushed strongly, carrying with it everything that was in its way, though they didn't notice. Water rose and fell violently. The sound of its crashing reached higher and higher; they thought it would swallow them. Then they were embraced in a deep silence and water passed beneath them, slithering away like a mythical snake suddenly leaving the depths of the mountain after having been imprisoned for centuries. It started to crush everything.

"We're like that water. We don't know what is being swallowed in front of us, but we just keep going. Because we're together, we're not afraid. We don't care, then we crash. It's just the beginning, and beginnings are always violent. Everything is permitted and legal. And as long as, in the end, we water the fields and give the desert a great green carpet of happiness, our rush will not continue for long. We will calm down after a while, but we will give the soil a different color! A different life."

Silence continued, the moon was kind, the flood passed away.

ع   ع   ع

"But what about her? Did you write anything?"

The young man said, "I tore up everything. How would I send my letters? Aden is far away now. How stupid I was. I said, I'll write her all the time. Perhaps she thinks I'm a hero now and waits for me to tell her stories about my adventures. She wouldn't believe that I tremble when I hear gunfire, as if the bullet had entered deep inside me. You're older than me, you've seen many vast horizons. Perhaps you're making fun of me now…But I…"

He laughed sadly and went on.

"I'm just a kid. I only know math and writing and talking about patriotism. The biggest thing in my life is the fact that I'm here. I made this decision without thinking. If I had thought for just a moment, I wouldn't be here—it's just the excitement of it all. I talked about patriotism until people couldn't bear to hear anymore…now and here is the revolution. How far away from it am I? Everyone said 'Volunteer, volunteer,' and so I volunteered. I'd only been married a few months. I didn't think of my bride. Her father told me, 'Don't worry, I'll be here.' My friends said, 'We'll be here.' And here I am. She would be ashamed of me, if I told her what war is and what fear is. I say to myself, I'm afraid for her sake, but I'm a liar. I taste my desire for life at each and every shot."

Another shot sounded. He trembled, and his throat was dry.

The sailor said, "I hope he was hit. They're so wicked. They know that the moonlight uncovers the peaks, and then they can climb the rocks and search for openings. But he fell down. Is something wrong?"

"No, no. I'm scared to death."

"Don't say that. Keep on talking as if nothing happened."

"You're a different kind of person from me. You fought today and before today, probably more than once."

The sailor laughed, "On many a side and without any reason. But today, I'm fighting for something. Perhaps I fought before with the Italians and after that I fought with the English, and then I was an arms smuggler. But I didn't feel anything. Then, neither the mountains nor the stars nor even the color of rain, nothing in the world excited me. I used to dream about this, this cold air, these naked peaks. Those stupid infiltrators, hunters of gold, and arms, and stupidity! Those dreamers of the revolution and the holiday commemorating it. I dreamt of all of them. I didn't know that under this rain, my country's rain, I'd be a hunter. Yes, my son, I knew streets in ports all over the world. I slept on their pavement. I was a beggar in the narrow streets of Marseilles. I was hungry. I worked days and nights. I worked in coal mines, near the flames of ovens and under an icy cold sky. I knew what it means to fight a war that is not your war. It's difficult to see hungry faces and now, don't you want me to shout happily here, 'I'm so happy, I'm so happy!' I'll tell this to all the people everywhere. Oh. How ashamed I was to tell them where I'm from, but now, I won't be ashamed at all, but I'll tell them your story. The son of Aden, who sits nearly naked and hungry on the peak of mountains, in a cold whose taste he doesn't know, eating only dry bread, and dreaming of grilled rabbit, writing imaginary letters to an imaginary woman."

"I'm not lying."

"I didn't say you were. Everything here is real, to the degree that reality isn't believable anymore!"

Their eyes searched for something in front of them, something other than silence or the color of rain, something that felt like feet creeping, like a sharp arrow planting death. The valley under them looked far away, it had lost its imaginary strength. It calmly led southward. Nobody knows where that valley starts or ends. Even if they knew it wouldn't matter, what's important is that it provides. The creeping sound got closer, closer, and the color of the moon became more yellow.

The sailor said, "Something happened in a port. I was a young man with some green and red banknotes in my hands; inside me masculine impulses were erupting; I hadn't yet sold my strength to anybody. I worked honorably, by sweat and hard work. I was happy that I'd left Yemen behind me to see a new world full of lights and noise and people. The least of these I thought were angels. On that night, in that port, I lost my virginity in the arms of the first woman I met. She had a baby, I gave her generously all my money. I took from her more than my manhood. She told me lots of things, but I didn't understand anything. I had a fever. I'd spent six months on board the ship. Do you know the meaning of that kind of loneliness? I didn't know until then, but I found it in the bed of that woman on that night, when I discovered her kisses were false. I didn't realize that until I returned to sea, when I reflected on my memories. I knew then that I was stupid, but I didn't forget that port. I sent letter after letter to her, even though I had forgotten her name; all I remembered was the name of the port, and that was enough for me to love her. I've returned many times, but she wasn't there. I returned to her after three years. That was the only thing I called love. I knew that she cheated me; she took everything, every-thing, but left me the sourness of loneliness. She planted this sourness, yes, she planted it. Oh, friend, you own a home, have love and friends, but me? I've returned to Yemen after twenty years. I've been changed somewhat. I tried to go back to the sea, that big friend that I've not missed, the one who's always ready to embrace me at any moment. And now you see me here and then there. It's just chance, isn't it? A chance, or the luck that I've always wanted. I've sold myself for more than an army, a company. I've learned how to work in a ship and learned how to hold a gun and kill people I don't know, with whom I have no personal argument. But today, it's a different matter; I know for the first time why I'm here, why I hold this gun in my hand. I may not know who I am killing, but I know why I kill. Do you hear me? After twenty years, for the first time, I know some-thing. The picture of graveyards is still in front of me. I returned carrying gifts and money, but I found only tombstones before my eyes. Here, I'm also carving new tombstones, perhaps I'll make one for myself."

The other voice interrupted him suddenly, and said, "Please don't say that…"

"Morning is getting close, we'll stay here together."

"Yes, we will, we're the only ones left."

"Nobody knows, perhaps there are others who, like us, could've made their way to these rocks."

"Maybe."

From far away a light appeared, but the moon had not yet disappeared. In the distance before the two men, the horizon connected with the earth. There was a delightful smell.

"Look, it's the rain, don't you see its color? I can't describe it, but I feel it in a strange way, so much I can almost describe it…"

"I can feel its smell, a fragrance I used to sell in a store I worked in…"

The creeping sound got closer, the ground announced it. Light covered both of them, voices rose and there were several shots, fire, light, dust around them. The valley echoed with the sounds…

"Don't be afraid, we'll stay together."

"And you'll tell this story on the ship."

"Yes, I'll tell them about the color of rain in my home country."

"I'll tell them in Aden, what cold tastes like."

The mountain rang with the noise of moving water roaring into the valley, gunfire was all around them, and the sounds—of shots and the rushing water—echoed and re-echoed through the mountain passes.

The Saturday Market

When the car broke down at the end of Sumaytah valley, we had to walk the rest of the way to the Saturday Market.

I loved the walk, especially when we crossed a stream with cool running water. A gentle breeze blew, and before us stood the lofty and rocky Hujariyyah mountains, embracing villages, and green land rich with growing wheat.

Sumaytah valley is beautiful in the evening when quiet comes, when the sun has sunk away gathering its bloody rays behind it, and the sound of water sings a sad Yemeni song.

But I'm angry now, because the weather is hot, the sun strong, and the water tasteless. The faces of fellow travelers are tired and yellowish. Tomorrow is the *Eid* (feast), and we have to reach our villages tonight. Ever since yesterday, when we left Aden, each of us has been dreaming of a festive evening party with our wives and children.

But the cursed car broke down.

After we spent four hours waiting near the car that refused to start, we could no longer avoid the walk. We were hungry, our stomachs churned violently, encouraging us to keep moving, especially when one of us reminded the other that it was Saturday, the day the market is filled with all sorts of things.

I put a head cover on to protect my head from the sun. I raised my sarong to my knees and splashed strongly through the water while looking at the mountains and trees, listening to the lowing of cows tromping about nearby in the valley and a skinny dog barking. I looked in the eyes of the farmers who lazily followed our pedestrian caravan.

The market was not far away.

As we were leaving the valley and had walked for a while, we noticed a green meadow and some huts made of wood and dry straw, under which sat the sellers. Even from the distance, you could hear their voices and the voices of buyers. Falcons soared high, going round and round over the slaughterhouse at the other end of the market. Donkeys brayed, sending mating calls to each other. Then a rotten smell filled the air as children shouted and threw scraps of rotten fruit at each other.

As I reached the market, I dropped into the nearest seat in the café and started to guzzle down hot coffee. The market was big. Nearby was a hill with a British flag raised, a white building, a camp, and an armed guard in his police uniform.

Saturday Market is the border point between North and South Yemen. At the bottom of the hill an infinitely green valley extends, which is crossed by Sumaytah valley that descends from the Hajariyyah mountains. When it rains, the gushing water flowing from the north carries mud, trees, and cars that chose the heart of the valley for a road; it carries people as well and whatever else stands in its way. The silent valley does not salute anyone. It is silent like death when it embraces its victims. Oh! How much life has been snuffed out silently by the valley.

The hill still remembered, until only recently, the English bullets harvesting revolutionaries from the Subayha tribe. The avenging bullets are fired silently every evening. Oh, you valley of Sumaytah, when will you be silent?

Each of my friends went his own way once we reached the market. I relaxed under the roofed cafe, looking around me. There was a noisy mill in front of me. Nearby was the donkeys' pen. Those donkeys carried the grain to the mill; they were not headed for the slaughterhouse and its horrid stench, the smell of blood and other filth that spattered onto the slaughterhouse floor. Flies buzzed and falcons descended from their heights to attack the fleshy scraps scattered all over the slaughterhouse. Women, in their clothes as black as their faces, were selling fruit and vegetables. Their voices could be heard above with their muffled coughs. The market was filled with the sounds of buyers and sellers, the screeches of falcons, and the buzz of flies pestering people's eyes and mouths at every turn.

I was thinking about my wife, whom I would see in a couple of hours, and my son, who was born while I was abroad, and about all of the little things I dreamed of under that roofed passage, while the hot noon sun poured down on our heads. How badly I wanted to be at home with my wife at this very moment.

Tomorrow was the feast. The market with its noises was disturbing me. So, too, were the shouts and sounds of animals, and the braying of male donkeys as they tried to get the attention of female donkeys in front of the mill; ropes around their necks tying them to the wall prevented them from doing what they liked. The battle between the donkeys and the ropes was great.

The sun was beating down strongly, and flies attacked our eyes constantly. A woman near me was scrutinizing her surroundings. She was a young, tanned, thin woman in a black dress. Her face showed signs of poverty suffered during her youth. As she followed what was going on around her, she groaned in despair whenever the donkeys were prevented from doing what they desired. I looked hard at her, all the while the mill producing an unbearable noise. What was she thinking? And what was I doing here? It seemed we both thought of one thing: of the battle that was not yet over for the donkeys. They were struggling, even if they could not move from the spot where they were tied. It was their fate to be tied up with ropes. They knew what they wanted, but could not get it, as long as the ropes held them back. Their eyes were absent in a daze.

The noonday sun was burning the ground, cars droned through the market on their way to the military camps, their passengers, red-faced soldiers, were sweating profusely. The woman waited. My nerves were about to snap. I was thinking about my life, the life of the market, the woman, the donkeys, and the battle that the woman finally ended by suddenly untying their ropes. Then she sat at a distance to watch, as we exchanged a knowing look.

And those in the market, what were they thinking about?

Suddenly, the horn sounded in the military camp. But, the woman still sat in the shadow of the mill, breathless…

∾ ∾ ∾

I dreamed about how comfortable my room would be tonight. From the middle of the market, the sound of a flute rose, accompanied by a drum and a Tuhami song and a dance by a young brunette, her hair the color of mud from the valley floor on a flood day. Her black glittering eyes winked, and the movements of her exciting sexy body and her half-opened mouth and her tongue as it darted over her full lips made me withdraw in a whirl of need.

The donkeys, the woman out of breath, and I were all possessed by dread. There was a young woman in her thirties with shining eyes and another young woman in her twenties dancing with a call in her black eyes, her lips a sin, and her body a hell of lust. I had to run away to escape.

I walked away from the roofed cafe and walked round and round in the market like a madman, colliding on my way with skinny, blue-faced children with bare feet, and women with oil dripping from their hair over their faces under the strong sun. The oil contorted their already-ugly faces.

A smelly man grabbed me by the hand, begging me to buy something from his store. A child with tears in his eyes ran behind me extending his hand towards me, his lips mouthing a painful request. A servant carried a half-sleeping and half-dead child. His face shouted of pain and sickness.

Even the animals on sale in the market were sick. I was mechanically chewing some qat and smoking. I was searching for a way to get to my own village before sunset. When I returned to the roofed passageway, the woman had left, carrying a big jute sack on her head, the noon sun frying her naked feet. Sumaytah valley was burning the green meadow not far away from the rocky Hujariyyah mountains that embraced all the houses, the countryside, and the hordes of people carrying bundles on their backs.

Abu Rupee

A few raindrops were dripping in front of the store as I stood shivering from the cold. But the rain didn't bother me; what worried me was—why was he late? On the wall near the store, I noticed a drawing he had done yesterday. The drawing smiled. Abu Rupee was such a nice guy.

I sat down on the stairs of the store and thought about Abu Rupee.

Three years ago, while I was sitting in the small plaza in front of our store, he came walking slowly by, looking at the ground, kicking stones with his foot. You could tell somehow he was deep in thought. When he looked up and saw me, he smiled. "May I sit down?" he asked.

I laughingly looked at him and said, "Why not, it's God's plaza after all!"

He shook his head, astonished, looking at the plaza and me.

"Is there anything left in this world that belongs to God? I'm amazed to hear you say that. People have taken everything that belongs to God. This plaza belongs to the government, and you represent the government."

I laughed. How could I, a kid still in elementary school, represent the government? What a funny idea!

"Have a seat, Abu Rupee."

"How do you know my name?"

"Is there anyone in Addis Ababa who doesn't know your name?"

He sat by me and began drawing lines on the ground with his small cane. They looked strange at first, but soon became a funny picture.

He took a deep breath as he looked at what he drew. "Listen, what's your name?"

"Sa'id."

"Do you study at the community school?"

"Yes, I'm in the fifth grade," I said proudly.

Abu Rupee was thirty-five, with a brown face, deep eyes, and a mysterious smile, which seemed to mock people. "Listen, Saʿid, can you see what I drew?"

"A donkey."

He hit me gently on my back and said: "Look carefully."

At first it appeared to be nothing more than a donkey, but his head was odd; it didn't look like a donkey's head; it seemed to be the face of someone familiar.

"It's Bajahsh!" I said and I laughed. The drawing looked just like him.

"But why is he a donkey?" asked Abu Rupee.

"His name means a young donkey," I answered, "and he *is* a donkey, too. He wouldn't give me a rupee yesterday."

Abu Rupee was quiet for a moment and then said: "What do you want to be when you grow up?"

Quickly I replied: "A merchant."

"Now, *you're* a donkey; don't you know that merchants are bad people—do you want to be a bad person?"

"No, I want to be a merchant so I can help the poor."

"Son, all of them said that they wanted to help the poor when they were young like you. Today, they've got lots of money and have forgotten the people, forgotten all about the poor." And he continued to say: "Listen, I'm going to draw something else for you, would you like that?"

"Oh. Yeah!"

His cane drew quickly on the ground. Moments later there were mountains, a sun, people, more donkeys, and other things that I could not distinguish.

"What is this, Abu Rupee?"

"Your homeland."

He continued to draw and draw as sweat glazed his face. Then I saw a tear run down his cheek. His eyes stared hard at the picture he had drawn. Suddenly he turned to me and pointed to the distance. "Do you know that your country is out there? It's beautiful, all of it, its mountains, trees, sun, and valleys. How would you know though, you're still young. Have you ever been to Yemen?"

"No."

"How would you know then? Listen, you've got to go to Yemen. What are you doing here in the land of other people?"

I didn't answer. I knew the land of my father was far away. I've heard my father talk about my grandfather, whom I've never seen, and about my brothers, whom I haven't even met. Also, I've heard my father's friends talk about many things: gold, newspapers, and things I couldn't understand. I whispered to Abu Rupee, saying, "Listen, Abu Rupee, what do the newspapers say?"

He hit the ground with his cane and quickly said, "What do we have to do with the newspapers? All of them are liars, son, don't believe them; they're greedy, they run after money. If you've got money they try to get what you've got, but if you don't have any, then no one will even say hello to you. Saeed, listen, why do all Yemenis emigrate? Why? They're afraid. They couldn't stay in their country so they ran away, left it to the bastards. Nobody knows exactly when they started emigrating. Maybe a thousand years ago, maybe more. The legends, they say, tell us that the Ma'arb Dam was destroyed by a small mouse. What liars! They're the ones who destroyed the dam with their corruption. And later they couldn't rebuild it, so they ran off. God said: 'There was in Saba two gardens, one to the right and one to the left. Eat of the sustenance provided by your Lord, and be grateful to Him. It is a territory fair and happy, and a Lord oft-forgiving!' Saeed, we had a good land, and Balqis—did you ever hear of Balqis? You're probably still too young, but when you get older you'll understand everything. Balqis was the first woman, in the world, chosen by her people to lead their country. Look where we are now, how far our civilization has come. We've left our country and our women behind.

He sighed deeply and said: "Oh, we left to look for other people's riches, even though our own land has gold. God said in the Quran there is no place better than our country. It's a paradise in need of its own people, its own men."

Abu Rupee and I became friends. Sometimes, we went together to rich people's houses to draw their portraits on the walls. One was drawn like a ram hitting a rock with his horns. We would sit back and watch people laugh as they looked at the drawings.

"You know, Saeed, if I went to Yemen, I'd be very rich."

"And would you forget the poor?"

He laughed and said: "No, I wouldn't forget them. In Yemen, one is in his own country, but here we're in another people's land. We're foreigners. It is shameful for them to look at us and say, 'Look at the Yemeni, he walks barefooted and wears rags.' But what can we do? God gave the rich hearts of stone."

And we said goodbye that night.

Despite our friendship I didn't know where Abu Rupee lived. Whenever I asked him, he would answer: "God's land is vast and wide."

"But you said that the people had taken God's land."

"That's right. Don't be upset; the Government's land is vast and wide."

Abu Rupee drew particularly well the people he hated. He once told me, "Do you know that Bajahsh gave me five rupees today?" and then proudly added, "but I refused, so people won't say that Abu Rupee is greedy. I took only one rupee from him."

જ   જ   જ

The rain fell continuously. The drawings on the wall looked like they were crying with the rain. The street was empty, except for some taxis hurrying through the downpour.

Where did Abu Rupee go? Something must have happened to him. In the past three years, he had never disappeared like this. Once before, he had been absent, but that was because he was sick. He had lost so much weight, he looked as thin as his cane. Pale and weak, he had come to me, explaining where he'd been. His voice still echoes in my memory, as he said, "What can we do? God inflicts illness on us. Here we are, not a cent to our names, and he goes and adds sickness to our poverty!"

"But, Abu Rupee," I asked, "why don't you work?"

"Son, you're still young, you don't understand. Don't I work every day? I thought you were smart enough to understand. Don't you know what art means? Listen, drawing is an occupation, the best in the world."

"Yeah, but it doesn't feed you."

"So, who wants to eat? What's important is that people are happy when they see my drawings. People want to say to this merchant or that one that he is an ass or a dog, but they can't. I draw what I want, no one can say a word."

"Why not?"

"You know, when you tell someone that he's a dog, he gets upset. But when you draw him as a dog or donkey, people will laugh, and he's not upset. This is human nature. You're still young, but when you get older you'll understand what I'm talking about."

But Abu Rupee didn't come back. A week passed and most of his drawings were erased from walls except for a small picture he had drawn for me.

When he drew that one, he had asked me: "What do you want to be when you grow up?"

"An artist," I replied quickly.

It was a picture of me, holding a brush. Under the picture, Abu Rupee had written his name. Suddenly, I heard my father's voice, "What's wrong with you? Every day you come here and stand in the cold. Come in, or I'll come and get you…"

But I looked around sadly. As I entered the store, I turned to my father who was busy balancing his accounts. "Where's Abu Rupee?" I asked quietly.

"They've deported him."

"Where to?"

"To Yemen."

"But why?"

"Because he's crazy."

❧   ❧   ❧

Five years later, I left Addis Ababa for Aden. While I sat sipping tea in a noisy café in the Sheik Othman neighborhood, I suddenly saw him coming in. Quickly I shouted, "Abu Rupee! Abu Rupee!"

He turned toward me, but before I could stand up to embrace him he had run away. I ran behind him, but he was lost in the crowds. His clothes were torn, his feet bare, and I had seen traces of misery on his face.

The café owner said: "Where do you know him from? They call him the Madman here. Every day he draws on walls, pictures of people that look like dogs."

"But he's not mad," I said.

"If he is not mad, then why doesn't he look for a job to fill his stomach…"

I stood there, silent.

The Slap

Raindrops were falling on the doors of our store. The ground of the road seemed to greet those drops kindly. Black ghosts cloaked in white moved quickly back and forth in front of the store and vanished around the street corner.

I looked at the street, where fast cars mingled with horse-drawn carts. The horses were rushing forward under the lashes of the drivers' whips; white, steamy breath puffed from the horses' mouths.

Do I tell him now, or should I wait until morning?

I looked around. My father sat in an old armchair next to me. Using an old pair of scissors, he was busily cutting up cardboard boxes to make covers for books and notebooks. In his mouth was a big ball of qat which he quickly chewed and then sucked out what his teeth juiced from the wad.

I looked out to the street once again. I couldn't stop thinking about the school principal's orders to all of us. There would be severe punishments to the pupils who did not comply.

The heat of the qat leaves that he had been chewing since early afternoon now seemed to seize my father. If I told him the news now, I thought, he would surely answer with a slap or a kick. I looked at him, thinking about how hard he could hit me. I saw his hands cutting the cardboard boxes, and the bulging veins, which looked as though they were about to explode. Drops of sweat shone on his forehead. The cold made me shiver as a draft blew in from the street.

There was no need to tell him now. I would wait until tomorrow morning when he woke up and that big wide smile of his, which had now disappeared behind his stern look, would return to his lips.

I was a skinny eleven-year-old in the fifth grade. As the cold breeze blew, I felt a chill; I shivered from cold and fear mixed together. I was afraid to tell my father what the principal asked—he would punish me. I was also afraid of not telling him—then the principal would punish me. I'd rather have my father's punishment, which I'm used to, especially his slaps.

My father kept doing what he was doing, the cardboard sheets falling in square and rectangular shapes from between his hands. He never made a mistake at this job.

The raindrops stopped falling and the sun came out again, but its rays were faint and far away before it disappeared.

Those weak yellow rays could not keep away the darkness of night, which began to fall on the town.

At that moment, one of those black ghosts wrapped in white entered the store. The ghost was tall and his cheeks were frozen from the cold. He sucked on his lips and coughed.

He looked at me and at the goods in the store and said: "I want to buy a large number of notebooks, so I hope you can give me a good price."

As I laid out a pile of notebooks, my father, caught up in his work, raised one eyebrow, peering over at the customer standing in front of me. While the man chose what he wanted, I tried to get my father's attention to show him that I was a skillful salesman and that I had talked to the man, offering him the largest quantity I could find. The man smiled and coughed saying, "You Arab kids..."

My father heard the man cough. He looked at the stranger's sunken cheeks and yellowish face, and said in Arabic: "Sa'id, don't get close to the man, he has tuberculosis."

The word paralyzed me. I looked at the man, scared. Does he carry death inside him? I turned to my father, alarmed. But he was still working, the veins in his hands swollen even more as he kept cutting with the scissors, and the squares and rectangles of cardboard fell on the floor. I looked at the man again and felt frightened as I got closer to him. He was quiet, smiled at me, then chose what he wanted.

I told him the price, the words tumbling out of my mouth, trying to get rid of him as soon as possible. When he paid the money, I relaxed, then quickly gave him the change and sat down. But the man did not leave. He looked at the money I had given him and then looked back at me. Gently he said, "My son, you've made a mistake, you've given me too much change." He gave me back some money.

My father heard the man. He got up from his seat, thanked the man, and put the money in the cash register.

I watched the man leave the store, his coughing echoing behind him. Then he turned to spit on the street, red spit, which disappeared with the running rainwater on the ground. My father did not go back to his work. Instead, he stood in front of me, tall and strong as he raised his hand and hit me. I fell on the floor with the sound of his slap thundering in my ears.

His lips were moving, but I couldn't hear a thing. I didn't cry, because I was used to being slapped. What really hurt, was that I remembered the principal's threats. How could I tell my father *now*? The echoes vanished gradually and I started to hear words coming from his mouth: "You kids today. You'd sell the entire store for one cent! You can't even add right. So, tell me, why do I send you to school every day? Why do we do that? Is it so you can play, or become a man?"

His hands returned to the work of cutting up the cartons, but only after leaving red fingerprints on my face.

The qat ball disappeared in his mouth as he swallowed hard. He continued, "I wish our fathers could have given us an education. You should thank God that you go to school every day and have someone to give you food and drink and pay school tuition. When I was your age, we used to work and provide for our parents. We even left our country and traveled to other countries to work, and all of this was so that life would be good for you..."

The echoes returned to my ears. My father's words were lost, those words I knew quite well. My fear of the principal grew. It was getting colder, or perhaps the sun had just disappeared into the dusk. There was no sign that the sun had ever existed, except for a red glow on the faraway mountains surrounding Addis Ababa. I was shivering from the cold, except for my cheek that still throbbed from the slap. The store was quiet, except for the sound of the scissors busy snipping squares and rectangles.

All my fears returned. I imagined the school principal with his Sudanese accent and red eyes, his short fat body as he threatened the students every morning when they arrived without the uniforms that he stipulated. His threats had become louder lately, because the anniversary of the emperor's coronation was getting closer. He wanted us to dress extra nicely in uniforms. He threatened to lock us down in the school's dank basement, with the hungry snakes and scorpions. We knew the principal. He did not lie. He would carry out his threats happily. The echoes of my father's words completely vanished. In the shop, I could hear only the sound of the scissors as they sliced cardboard under my father's strong fingers and spit squares and rectangles out of their jaws.

I forced my eyes to look at my father's face, which was glazed over with a terrible look. Where was his sweet smile *now*?

In the morning, I saw my father smiling. Then when he looked at my face, he said: "What's wrong with your cheek?"

I did not answer. I gave him a deep look, reminding him of what had happened yesterday. I felt his fingers passing gently over my head, and then he kindly rubbed my shoulder and said, "Son, you have to learn. What else can we do? We have to do what has to be done."

It was the perfect opportunity to ask him; I blurted out, childishly: "Daddy, all the students have bought new school clothes; I'm the only one who hasn't. Do you want them to talk about me?"

Minutes later we walked out together to buy what I needed.

The Last Class

The classroom was quiet, and the thirty students breathed gently as they anxiously watched the door. Any moment now, the teacher would enter to teach his last class.

Any other day, at such a moment, the classroom would be a complete mess with students throwing chalk and calling each other names. You might find one of them in a corner, stuffing his mouth with a piece of bread, while hungry eyes followed his hand as it moved to his mouth. Another student, standing on a chair in front of the blackboard, would be trying to write down some fleeting thought in weak, tiny handwriting, while another laughed as he corrected his mistakes. But as soon as the teacher would enter the classroom, the noise would suddenly calm down and the students rush back to their seats. Quiet would take over, and the students' eyes would become anxious and worried. They were eyes that knew their own guilt, but within seconds after the teacher left, they would return to what they had been doing.

&ep; &ep; &ep;

But today was very different. Everybody sat quietly, in deep silence, with their small eyes looking questioningly at the door, then the blackboard, and the teacher's empty chair.

Today, all of the sixth-grade class shared the same feeling, a feeling of real anxiety. They were dreading this last class.

A year before a young teacher, about twenty-six years old, had entered their classroom. He had a small moustache and reading glasses, under which appeared his young dreamy eyes, which were strong and self-assured. He had a small bald spot that was slowly taking over his yet-black head of hair. On that day he had been a stranger, but soon he became very close to the students. They could not have imagined that one day they would be sitting in this silence, like that of a funeral, to say goodbye with due respect and anger. Why? Yes, why should they have to say goodbye? They loved him more than they loved the school itself. His was the only class in the whole school that no student wanted to miss.

His words always came from the heart in a quiet, wise and deep voice that settled in those small hearts filled with love for life. This teacher had opened their hearts to a wide world. For the first time and from his lips, they heard new words: the people, the nation, the homeland, and how they should love all these. True, they had heard the same words from other teachers and from their parents when they read the newspaper. But he had added beautiful new meaning to these words.

Their eyes were still fixed on the door. The teacher had not come yet. They felt for the first time that they needed him, needed his talks, his sad voice. Why was he late? They had never once wanted him to be absent. They couldn't believe that he would ever leave them, especially not today, and possibly forever. They wouldn't see him after today in their classroom. They wouldn't hear his voice.

He softly opened the door. Nobody noticed when the teacher entered, nor did he notice at first when the students stood up to salute him. He entered quietly and looked at all of them with a sad smile and tired eyes. Moments passed. In those moments the teacher's eyes met each student's eyes in a silent salute.

"Sit down...sit down."

But the students continued to stand. The teacher smiled. They all sat down and so did he.

❧ ❧ ❧

Memories rushed back to the students all anew of the first day when he had entered the classroom. They had heard a lot about him even before he became their teacher. They had heard about him and read about him before they saw him.

They were very happy when they knew that he would be their history teacher. He had entered the classroom that day with a smile on his face. It was not the same as the sad one they saw on his face today. They remembered very well how he had started their first lesson. He had talked to them like a brother, a big brother who did not insist on their respect, but instead they found themselves respecting him, as he wrote with elegant handwriting on the blackboard, "The History of Yemen."

He did not talk to them about what was written in schoolbooks but told them new things about ancient civilizations, about the authenticity of a people who created civilizations and built dams and established a home country in a small paradise, who built Arabia Felix, the original name for Yemen.

From the ancient history to the present one, he gently talked about their country divided into a north and a south.

Here they were today, meeting for their last class, in their small classroom with its old walls and wide windows. The memories of a whole year flooded his heart and mind and the hearts and minds of every student. On the ceiling, the fan quietly turned round and round.

A Woman

It was nighttime. We were walking with slow, fearful steps, looking ahead with empty gazes, searching for some unknown thing. We had nothing particular in mind.

We walked, attracted by the silence of night and the darkness of the small alleys that we passed. All we heard was the sound of our feet as they sank in the mud from the morning rain.

The laughter of drunken men and prostitutes and the light coming from bars heated the blood in our veins, despite the cold air that penetrated our bodies.

We were four. Ahmed Ali, the eldest among us, was nineteen years old, his light-brown face lit with shining eyes. He talked a lot about women and shivered whenever he heard a woman's voice. By his side, Numaan walked while attentively listening to what Ahmed Ali was saying. He also shivered as he looked hungrily into the lighted doors in that alley and kept saying, "Huh, huh! And what else?"

And Fatso—with his big body that didn't suit his age—sixteen years old, panting, trying to keep up with us. Sweat was pouring out of him and his mouth was wide open as if he wanted to swallow the air all in one gulp. He shouted for us to wait for him. As for me, I was the youngest, fourteen years old, skinny, a fast walker. I was looking curiously in the bars that we passed, trying to see what went on behind those doors. I ached when I heard women laughing or glimpsed the shadows of their bodies inside the bar, as they danced and sang.

Darkness enveloped the alley and our feet kept sinking in the mud. Ethiopian music emanated from the bar; the sound of musical instruments pulled our bodies towards that unknown something we were in search of. Our blank gazes seemed to penetrate the darkness, helping us find our way so that we wouldn't collide with the drunken men and women. We tried to walk in the shadows and hide as much as we could, so none of our relatives or friends would see us. Merely being seen at this time of night, in such a neighborhood in Addis Ababa, would raise a lot of eyebrows.

Our group came to a stop in one of the alleys and Ahmed said, as he pointed: "Listen, Qassim, take off your hat. If we bump into anyone who knows us, we'll say that someone snatched your hat and ran off with it and now we're trying to find him."

Everyone nodded in agreement. I was the youngest, and so I had to do what they said. I pulled my hat off and tucked it into one of my pockets. Then we kept walking, searching for what, we did not know.

It was very cold, and desire burned violently inside us. We would shake and tingle all over whenever Ahmed talked about women.

The moon rose from behind the accumulating clouds in the dreamy sky of Addis Ababa. It lit the way in front of us so that we could see the pools of water and the mud that covered the floor of the alley. Ghosts moved furtively, going to an unknown place they might have known, or did not know. Noisy music was playing in the small bars; we felt it was satanic music to excite the animal lust about to explode within us.

From other bars came mysterious, quiet, and divine music that gave us a feeling of tranquility; but still our lust could not be quelled.

At the head of the alley a white ghost suddenly appeared, a ghost which quickly moved that quickly toward us. We stopped, to peer at it more closely.

The ghost was a tawny-skinned woman, the color of coffee. She was short and voluptuous, with hair black as night, eyes shining in the misty darkness, framing her beautiful lips. She stopped when she saw us. The fat boy was blocking the way with his lumbering body. She smiled seductively and asked: "Huh, what do you want, young men?"

Ahmed, who had started to ache for a woman again, said: "Want to come with us?"

She smiled beautifully and asked: "Where are you going?"

"To your house," the fat boy said quickly and fearlessly, as more sweat poured down his face.

The woman answered, "Thank you, but I can't today. A man is already waiting for me tonight. But I can provide you with another girl."

Her smile widened as she winked adding, "She is more beautiful than I am, and even younger."

But no one said a word. We had surrounded her from all directions and she was trapped in the middle like a mouse. I trembled fitfully and was scared, but inside me was a hot fire was burning. Fearfully, I backed up several steps and looked at what was happening before me.

The woman did not try to move. She only looked at my friend sympathetically, for it seems she was used to this. Moreover, she was easily able to soothe children like us.

The fragrance of her perfume spread to my nose, fueling my excitement and increasing my sweat. I wanted to get close, but my feet were nailed to the mud.

My friends couldn't convince her, because they didn't know how. They insisted, however, that they would not go to anyone else.

It was a challenge for them.

The woman wanted to move on, but the three wild animals attacked her from every side, kissing and mauling her. She did not run or shout for help, but stood still for their hot kisses. She knew, somehow, that the young wild animals would not harm her or anybody else, for that matter. She was used to them. Well, my friends finally let her go. Then she turned and looked back at them. Her eyes held a strange seductive power, an irresistible force. As she was about to leave, she said: "Are you still insisting that you don't want another girl?"

All of them nodded their heads in silence.

She said: "Then, you'll find me waiting for you here, tomorrow."

The moon shone forth, its silver rays dispersing the heavy hateful clouds of Addis Ababa, uncovering the sky that hid behind them. I was trembling uncontrollably, my eyes eating the woman alive, her perfume tickling my nose while inside me a fire continued to burn.

She noticed me standing there. Her white teeth appeared, as her lips opened to smile. She said to me, as she pointed to my friends: "Why don't you join in?"

I didn't answer. I felt cold sweat breaking out all over me.

Her eyes widened with her smile: "You should take your share, too." She said. "You're a man, don't be afraid. Okay?...get involved, *mon petit!*"

She bent forward and kissed me on my lips. It was a long kiss, it was hot, I was ready to fall on my back. I felt her chest close to mine. Heat came from her chest, her young breasts seemed to pierce through me. She smiled as she saw the stupid smile on my face. Her eyes were full of tender kindness. She bent and kissed my face again, quickly. Those lips left fire all over me, and then she walked away.

For a long time I couldn't feel my feet touch the ground. My lips carried the warmth of her lips, my chest burned, and my cheeks were blazing. I felt very happy as I carried the traces of a woman on my body for the first time. Her fragrance was all over my clothes. My happiness was overwhelming. I remembered her eyes, and I felt something towards her—it was love. The following day, I crept back to the neighborhood, and I looked for that alley for a long time, but my efforts were in vain. I was sad, but my chest and lips could still recall the heat of lust that I had felt.

On dark nights, I still see her eyes shining through the darkness with love, kindness, and warmth.

On the Road to Asmara

It was an ordinary day, the sun asleep in the middle of the sky, its rays sprawled across the horizon like lazy arms. The sun lay sleeping over a thirsty land, the heart of the earth eager for water.

Clouds without rain floated above with dull pride. The earth stretched out its long asphalt tongue before us.

From the bar-restaurant, I looked out toward the horizon, bored. Perhaps the dust cloud meant that a car was coming. But, no vehicles appeared.

I checked the time. A woman in her forties was standing behind a bar, observing my anxiety. She smiled at me. A long time passed, or at least I felt like it had been a long time. I ordered a drink, but rejected an offer for dinner. I didn't feel hungry. It was three in the afternoon. Although it was the rainy season here in Ethiopia, no rain fell. A caravan of donkeys and half-naked men with hunger in their eyes were passing down the road. The men were leaning on canes to support their skinny, fatigued bodies. They threatened the donkeys with their canes.

The woman was looking at me, but we were the only people in the bar, with empty bottles and a swarm of flies. The road lay slumbering; inside it, laziness waited to be born. I didn't like waiting, but this lost city on the road had forced me to get out some qat and chew away the morning hours, waiting.

I had a strong impulse to leave the bar, but where would I go to?

I looked up and down the road, the caravan was moving between the old buildings lining both sides of the street. I started counting the flies, hoping to kill time. I looked at the clock.

"You keep checking the clock. Are you worried?"

I looked into her brown eyes.

"Do you have an important appointment in the capital?"

"Yes, I do."

I thought my words could not be heard, but her black ears picked out my whispers.

She was not beautiful, but in her eyes were traces of buried beauty. She was one of the leftovers of the Italian war. Everything here was old, even the women.

The sun along the road was cold. The people on it were lethargic, totally sapped of energy. Even the prostitute standing by her door. Boredom was killing her. She was looking down the road for customers. As for me, I'd had enough of that. There were more than ten doors, and lying behind them were beds with traces of their crimes. On the beds were women selling something to whoever knocked, their beds calling to everybody.

I counted the town's buildings: two stores, one on each side of the road, one of them closed, and four big luxurious bars, flies playing at their doors. The bars offered drinks, food, and a warm place to sleep with a lovely body.

I was anxious; the flies were bothering me. The woman next to me spoke. I was her only client since the morning bus had left town.

The donkey caravan was waiting in front of a small restaurant. The whole group went inside to eat something local and cheap.

At the edge of town, was a market. Men and women sat on the sidewalk, looking very sleepy. In front of them lay piles of eggs and crates of playful chickens. But there were no buyers.

"Why are you silent?"

In her eyes was something asking to be bought, though I wanted nothing but a ride to the capital. She stood and walked to the door. She was saying something, her shining white teeth appearing behind her full smile.

"The evening bus is late."

I didn't answer her.

"Perhaps it has changed its route!" she added.

She wanted me to stay there, but that was impossible. As much as I hated flies, I hated even more the thought of sleeping in small towns in the middle of nowhere on the road to Asmara.

I looked down at her legs—something attractive shone from them. Through her legs, I saw an old petrol station. The Italians had passed through here and left behind lots of things, including this woman. Black silky hair hung down over her back, and I had an acute desire to touch that hair.

"Aren't you hungry? I can get you a steak," she suggested.

She didn't look at me, but she continued.

"The sun doesn't burn; it's usually the rainy season now."

I looked at the sky—it was empty. A prostitute had left her room and walked over to the market. She was laughing. In the distance some dust rose up.

"No, that's not the bus—it's just a small car."

She was silent for a moment.

"You might have to sleep here!"

She returned to her place, on her lips a desire to talk. A dog barked when the donkey caravan left the restaurant. The travelers were wiping their mouths with their hands. Their faces gave the appearance of being fully satisfied, but their eyes were weeping.

The car passed by without stopping.

The woman sighed.

"It's a silly day, no work. Just another day!"

I left the bar, out of cigarettes. There was a kiosk; the man there had a piece of qat inside his mouth and various herbs in his lap.

"I want a pack of cigarettes."

He stood up to give me the pack. I tore the wrapper off. An oil truck pulled up in front of the bar; the driver was black. I smiled. For so long oil trucks had been driven only by Italians.

"I forgot the matches."

The man running the kiosk handed me a pack of matches and said: "Did you come to buy food?"

"No, I sold some food."

"Oh!" And he added after a moment, "The market is dead."

"Coffee has no value and grain isn't moving."

"The rain is late."

He realized that I was bored. He didn't move back to his place, but stood, watching me. I studied him, and my curiosity began to grow. He was not tall, and had some gray hair starting to show. His eyes were deep, his beard short against his cheeks. But he looked strong, and intelligence shone in his eyes.

"Are you from Asmara?" he said.

"Yes, but I work in Waissi," I answered.

"Are you going to the capital?"

I started liking him. I decided not to go back to the bar.

"Are there a lot of you here?" I asked.

"Who?"

"I mean Yemenis."

"Oh, there were lots of us when the Italians were here. But now there are only three of us. The owner of that closed store, another man who owns a mill nearby, and myself."

"Where did the others go?"

He shook his head sadly.

"Some died, some moved to the capital, a few returned back home."

"Just like that."

A moment of silence passed. A car passed, coming from the capital. The man continued, "This place was some town then, but today…even cars don't stop here, they just pass quickly through. Business is dead here."

"Why didn't you leave with the others?"

A smile appeared on his face, and something that was shining in his eyes dimmed a bit.

"Where to?"

I didn't answer. I didn't know how.

"I have nothing left but this store and a family. And sometimes I sell and buy food—that's when it doesn't rain."

I blew cigarette smoke into the air. The prostitute went back to her bed. I saw one of the market vendors looking lustfully at her. She was smiling now.

"Are you of mixed blood?" he asked.

I nodded.

"That's better than I am. At least you don't feel you're a stranger. You were born here."

"What about you?"

He closed his eyes. The qat leaves disappeared inside his mouth. I saw the face of a six-year-old girl peering through wooden boards stacked in the back of the store—behind the stock clearly lay living quarters. The child's eyes were beautiful, her black braids like silk, and there was something delightful about her demeanor.

"Daddy...Daddy. I want some mint candy," she said in Amharic.

"Come and get whatever you like," he answered back in Amharic.

She smiled and I saw her joyful white face once again before she disappeared between the boards, her smile lost in the open space. I heard her talking to someone in Amharic.

"Look, I've taken a whole bunch!" and she laughed.

"Doesn't she understand Arabic?"

He shook his head "No," and I didn't ask him why.

"It's four o'clock. Do you think there's any hope that the evening bus will come?"

"There's hope until five o'clock."

Two women crossed the street; they were coming toward us. They looked full of happiness and vitality. They were cracking jokes and one of them said laughingly: "Hey, you Arab, can we find a red handkerchief in your store?"

The man stood up lazily.

They had beautiful bodies, their legs long and shiny. One of them had firm young breasts. Lust spread with their perfume that filled the store. The man was trying to smile as he said: "I swear by your beauty, this handkerchief cost me a dollar and a half."

One of the women answered sweetly: "You want to profit from us!"

She winked as she said, "Come on, we're friends."

A terrible, bitter look came into his eyes.

The other laughed when her girlfriend whispered something in her ear. I looked quickly at my watch, my attention focused on the street.

A sexy voice rose and, with it, the lust of all the evils on earth. "Please, oh St. George, delay all the cars tonight."

I looked at them and said: "In that case, I'll sleep on the street."

They smiled, one saying as though pampering me, "Are you that stingy?"

The sexy voice said: "He's handsome and it seems that his pockets are full of money."

They paid for the handkerchief, but before leaving the store, the sexy voice said: "Our house is over there, the second door to the left. Don't forget, you will find there everything you need."

She winked, her laughter filling the quiet street.

God save us from such corruption. During the Italians' time there were lots of women like her, but then there was lots of work. But today there is too much corruption and no more work. Look at this street: there are more than ten whorehouses in addition to the bars.

A shadow near the store was from a large stone with an inscription in Latin, the name of a camp...1938. Sitting on the stone was an eight-year-old boy, laughing. He got up, marched away with a military march, and turned enthusiastically to give the store a salute. Then he smiled. His eyes were beautiful, but there was some sort of stupidity there. He kept his mouth shut to keep the flies from entering. I heard him murmuring something, then returned my attention to the store and the man.

"When did you come here from Yemen?"

He tried to remember and then said: "I think it was around thirty years ago. I was here before the Italians came. I worked with camel caravans for years. We used to carry arms to the coast, to the mountain region, and provide the Ethiopians with weapons to continue the resistance. The Italians killed our caravan leader. His name was Nu'man Saeed. We dispersed after his death. He was a very brave man, he didn't fear anyone. After the war, the Ethiopians rewarded us with prison." He shook his head from side to side as he recalled those memories.

"Life is still lovely...I've ended up here in this corner of the world. Thank God I wasn't lost like so many of my friends."

He was interrupted by a feminine voice calling from inside. It was an Ethiopian voice: "Oh, Hajji! Oh, Hajji! Where did your son go?"

He replied angrily: "Who am I? His guard to follow him everywhere?"

"Shame on you! Go fetch him before he gets lost or is hit by a car!"

He murmured something and said: "Problems…problems."

The boy was still playing on the stone, his dense eyes looking for something. The man shouted in Amharic: "Fatima! Fatima! Go and fetch your brother, wherever he is."

I saw the boy standing. With short shaky steps, he moved closer to the store.

"Hey!…what…who?" he stuttered.

The man was looking kindly at the boy.

"Where were you, Mansour? Do you want mint?"

The street cut through the heart of the long row of houses, where the prostitutes looked out with empty eyes. Again, there was no one in the streets.

"Is he your son?"

"Yes. He's a bit slow, but he goes to the Ethiopian school."

The child grinned foolishly and said: "Up…in the church…we went yesterday."

His younger sister came by and pulled him by the hand.

"Ouch…ouch. You're crazy," he said to her.

And he followed behind her, laughing.

"But why do you speak with them in Amharic? Isn't it better if you teach them Arabic?"

There was silence and sadness. The sun was setting. The sound of a car motor reached my ears.

"Everybody here speaks Amharic. With whom would they speak Arabic? We Yemenis here hardly get together. I'm tired and don't go to the capital much anymore. We all speak Amharic, the schools, too," and he laughed. "I personally have started to forget Arabic."

What he said was true. He used a lot of Amharic words when speaking with me.

The bus stopped in front of the store. I stretched my hand to wave goodbye.

"I wish you good luck."

He nodded his head thankfully and before I reached the bus, I turned to say: "Don't you ever consider going back to Yemen?"

He thought hard and then said: "Yemen. I have already forgotten it. All I'm waiting for is death. Nobody would know me there if I returned, and what would I bring back after being gone so long? No, I'll stay here until the end. There's nobody there for me anymore. I won't go back. My children might go back one day, when they realize that their father is a foreigner. But then they might not, they might stay as foreigners like me." Tears rolled down his face.

I started to leave, but something drew me to look at this short man with empty eyes and an empty smile.

His face appeared before my eyes, as the bus began to move down the long tongue of the street that stretched to the capital. The Italians had passed through here, as had the Yemenis on their camels. The cold sun was rising back up in the sky. The clouds filled and the rainy season fulfilled its promise. This sad street meant lost towns and lost people. One of them was lost, lost without hope in a small town on the road to Asmara.